The Fantasy Eaters

The Fantasy Eaters

Stories from Fiji

Subramani

An Original from Three Continents

©Subramani 1988

Three Continents Press
1636 Connecticut Avenue, N.W.
Washington, D.C. 20009

Library of Congress Cataloging-in-Publication Data:

Subramani.
    The fantasy eaters : stories from Fiji / Subramani. — 1st ed.
        p.   cm.
    "An original from Three Continents."
    Contents: Sautu — Tell me where the train goes — Groundlings — Tropical traumas — No man's land — Marigolds — Dear Primitive — Gamalian's woman — Kala — Gone bush.
    ISBN 0-89410-630-9.   ISBN 0-89410-631-7 (pbk.)
    I. Fiji—Fiction. I. Title.
PR9650.9.S84F36   1988
823—dc19   88-20030
                    CIP

All rights reserved. No part of this book
may be used or reproduced in any
manner whatsoever without written per-
mission from the publisher except for brief
quotations in reviews or articles.

Cover art and illustrations by Max K. Winkler
©Three Continents Press 1988

The Fantasy Eaters is a work of fiction.
All characters, places, and incidents are
fictional and therefore any resemblance to
actual persons, living or dead, or to places
and events, is entirely coincidental.

In the loving memory of my Mother

Table of Contents

Acknowledgments..ix

Sautu...1
Tell Me Where the Train Goes...11
Groundlings...19
Tropical Traumas...23
No Man's Land..29
Marigolds..39
Dear Primitive...47
Gamalian's Woman..55
Kala..63

Gone Bush (a novella)
   Artists of the Sea...77
   Karma in My Psyche..89
   Beginning of the End..123

Glossary..137
About the Author..141

Acknowledgments

Grateful acknowledgment is given to the following publications where stories in this collection first appeared:

Mana Publications: "Sautu," "Tell Me Where the Train Goes," "Tropical Traumas," and "No Man's Land";

Unispac: "Groundlings";

The Indo-Fijian Experience (ed. Subramani): "Marigolds";

South Pacific Stories (ed. Chris and Helen Tiffin): "Gamalian's Woman";

Kunapipi: "Dear Primitive";

Span: "Kala."

Some of these stories have also appeared in other publications and in translation. They were all written prior to the political developments which transpired in Fiji in 1987-1988, and are gathered here for the first time.

Sautu

That evening Dhanpat returned early from the mill barracks. Most of the night, lying on his string bed, he struggled with Kanga's remarks. He felt immensely uneasy and distressed.

His friend had brought out the tobacco and, wrapped up in their blankets, they filled their clay pipes and smoked. They talked of indenture, but the period was no longer clearly defined; it seemed like a labyrinth full of shadows and memories.

Then Kanga told him a story he had read in a Hindi paper. It was about an old Hindu who was afraid of dying. "Is it true," he asked Dhanpat, "that a man's memory sharpens before death?"

It didn't take long for Dhanpat to notice that his friend wasn't his usual self. He was less jocular and more introspective. Consequently there were long stretches of silence in their conversation when Kanga seemed tense and irascible one moment (the prattling of women and children next door seemed like an irritation grating on his nerves), and the next moment sank into a state of acute depression.

When Dhanpat saw him to bed, his friend held his arm and tried to talk. But Kanga's mouth merely opened and closed like that of a stranded fish.

Dhanpat couldn't sleep though he felt weary and his limbs ached. He coughed badly . After rubbing on some balm for pain, he slept. But not for long. Soon he was awakened by the barking of dogs and harsh whispers outside his hut. He went out with his lantern to see what was amiss: they were carrying Bansi's wife to the hospital.

And then he had those nightmares again: Ratni's madness, the pool of blood in dry sugar cane leaves, the frightening pursuit by apparitions on horseback, and Ratni's dismembered limbs in the machaan.

Dhanpat got up early. The minah birds were squawking angrily again on the bare branches of the tamarind tree. It made the cattle and goats restless. He donned his dhoti, picked his white cotton shirt, now coarsely patched and mildewed, from a nail, and staggered to the window to shoo the birds away.

Dulari was up early too; she was already milking the cows. After her mother Ratni's death, Dulari looked after the animals for her father. In return she took some milk for her baby.

A cloud had descended on Dhanpat's life after the simultaneous departure of Ratni and the children. Immediately after Ratni's death, Dulari was married. Then Dhaniram found work with a tailor and he shifted to town with his wife. And Somu disappeared from Sautu. With these exits a great deal of love was banished from Dhanpat's life.

When he had Ratni and the children, he saw the need for the body to be fine and the mind strong. Now his body was without motives or consequence. Detachment and acceptance of life came easily and quickly to him. He had read in the Gita: "Desire nothing so that you'll have everything." Once this was a line he quoted in mandali debates; now it was held with conviction.

The village was stirring again. It stirred only in the mornings and evenings with the departure and arrival of men from the fields and the sugar mill. The women hurried in and out of their huts, minding their orhini, while the bare-backed children squatted and rolled in the dirt yard.

Dhanpat had observed the unchanging life of the village for nearly fifty years. Sautu wasn't an old village. After indenture, a group of men and women scratched a little clearing from which the present squalid little huts sprang up.

The site was badly chosen. There were no rivers and the sea was thirty miles away. The village was hemmed in by an irregular stretch of unprosperous sugar cane fields in the south, and, in the north, by partly barren soapstone hills bearing occasional guava bushes and stunted rain trees and reeds.

Sautu was regarded as insignificant, and it turned its back on the world beyond. More thatch and bamboo structures appeared as the families became larger. They continued to till the obstinate earth; there was nowhere else to go. Besides, they were no longer moved by a momentum of their own. Habit and custom held them fettered to the place. Ultimately, Sautu, like its inhabitants, became an aberration, a contortion of history on that landscape.

Near the coast, in the west, there were several small Fijian villages. Much of the land was owned by local chiefs. When Dhanpat came with Ratni, who was in the late stages of pregnancy, he looked desperately for land on which to build a hut. The villagers counseled him to see Ratu Epeli who gave Dhanpat a plot at the edge of Sautu, and sent Tomasi to help build his hut.

Dhanpat's reverie was broken; a waft of breeze brought the damp odor of old hay and cow dung from the pen. He turned from the window and sat heavily on his string bed.

Now in disarray, his hut still retained signs of a past order in the faded limewash on matted bamboo walls, in the arrangenment of dull, discolored photographs, and ripped up crêpe on soap-box shelves.

The reeds in the roof had thinned and the walls sagged. Cobwebs hung in shabby strands from the rafters. The mud floor was uneven; where it was damp, the cow dung plaster had come off and the red earth showed.

It was always dismal and dark in the hut. The windows and doors rarely opened completely. The years had added nothing significant to his worldly possessions. A much-battered, tin suitcase under his string bed held his and Ratni's old clothes and odd cups and saucers, glass jugs, a large looking glass, and several combs and some jewelry—their wedding presents.

In a corner, where the wall and rafters were black with soot from the cooking, lay copper and aluminum utensils and earthenware. His broken dholak, brought from India, stood on an empty wooden box in another corner.

He looked reflectively at his earthly belongings; a great emptiness seemed to unfold within him.

Then he did something he hadn't done for a long time—he pulled out his suitcase and picked up the large jagged mirror, a gift from Kanga, and examined himself.

The piercing brown eyes, narrow and heavily wrinkled, the aquiline nose, and the thin line of his rather well-formed lips were the only visible parts; the rest of his face and head were concealed behind gray tangled hair.

Long years in the fields had bent his posture. His long and bony arms and legs were cracked and creased like the earth outside. He was reminded of Kanga—his withered and shrunken husk—and the mask of death on his face.

He felt old, exhausted, and bereft.

Ignoring the bowl of milk Dulari had left for him, he scrambled outside and went behind the hut to urinate.

Now slumped back against the wall of his hut, he watched the somnolent village minding its dull business.

He was relieved when Bhairo, the village barber, greeted him. He went inside the hut to get a mat. Bhairo pulled off his dusty canvas shoes, and squatted on the mat in the hot sun, resting his elbows on his scrawny legs.

"Acha, Dhanpat, I don't see you at mandali these days. Why?" he asked, fanning himself vigorously with his skull cap.

This was the correct way to begin. Bhairo knew it would lead, by way of discourse on comparative merits of illness and treatment, ancient and modern, to the scriptures. Bhairo trusted his own knowledge of Vedic literature and, secretly elated, he often embellished his arguments with learned quotations from the ancient books.

Bhairo, like most other villagers, respected Dhanpat less for his knowledge than for his common sense and fairness. But he was too much of a free thinker, too much at times like the despicable Samajis. No wonder, thought Bhairo, he bred a renegade—the highest form of delinquency, according to the Sautu norm—for a son.

Bhairo was disappointed when Tomasi appeared. He hurriedly opened his bundle and took out a wedding card for Dhanpat. It caught Tomasi's eyes.

"Aha, Bhairo. This modern thing catching fast. Where's the yellow rice?" asked Tomasi in broken Hindi.

Bhairo frowned. This wedding card was an odiously un-Hindu custom which he regretted but nevertheless propagated. But he understood well Tomasi's sinister fondness for asking awkward questions. He didn't answer.

Tomasi watched him and waited to be contradicted. Bhairo simply wilted under his stare, his face revealing the expression of self-denigration which unmistakably showed whenever he lost a verbal duel.

Bhairo resented the way Tomasi seemed to be appraising him. He resented most of all the way Tomasi's nostrils stared at him. Bhairo's effort to keep up an appearance of good companionship with Tomasi inevitably resulted in suppressed hostility.

He observed this at a Kali Puja. Bhairo was the protagonist in the rituals. He was in a trance, singing and dancing in complete abandon, round and round the grotesque brass idol. When he turned a corner, his eyes arrested a familiar figure in the crowd—a ponderous head with thick fuzzy hair and a dark face. And those nostrils—they stared at him. When their eyes met, Tomasi grinned. The trance was broken.

Bhairo gathered his bundle, nodded, and slipped away.

Dhanpat, however, derived a certain pleasure from Tomasi's friendly antagonism. Tomasi, eager to test Dhanpat's response to his newly-acquired ideas (from the visiting misnari), waited for an opportunity to begin. But today, scenting a certain dullness and abstract preoccupation in Dhanpat, he asked instead after Somu.

Somu was planning to come back. "Only for a visit. At Christmas," Dhanpat told his friends with a nonchalance which wasn't real. He hadn't told anyone, however, that Somu wanted to take him to Canada. He waited to burst it on them when it became a recognized and established fact.

Tomasi didn't take this aspect of Dhanpat's conversation seriously. He couldn't conceive of Dhanpat and Somu in any other setting. He was convinced that Somu was hiding in another village.

Tomasi flapped his large hands against his sleeveless blue coat in disappointment. For a moment he gazed, with a kind of proprietorial concern, at the sagging hut and the bare garden patch. The kassava sticks he had given Dhanpat for planting still lay under the tamarind.

Dhanpat anticipated Tomasi's half-patronizing, half-admonishing glance.

Tomasi stood there without saying anything while Dhanpat's mangy dog licked the sores on Tomasi's ankles. He crossed the yard to the tamarind fruits in various stages of decomposition. He examined a handful of fruits, dropped a couple into his coat pocket, and left.

In the pelting heat of the two o'clock sun, Dhanpat picked up his walking stick and turban, and headed for the village school. With his head slightly before his body, he walked as though hampered by a nagging problem.

He trudged on the ribbon of a well-beaten, dusty soapstone path, past the straggle of huts where women went listlessly about their tasks or sat under a mango or tamarind tree picking lice from their hair.

The huts looked desolate and the dirt yards showed ugly cracks. There were no gardens to speak of, no decorative trees except occasional marigold plants which bore small gaudy flowers. For the first time, Dhanpat was overwhelmed by the dereliction.

He rested for a while at Rambaran's store where the latter sold groceries from the front door and very bad rum from the back. Some men were drinking kava and smoking bidi cigarettes on the veranda. Two or three others were snoring on empty sugar bags. Rambaran was inside, in his black shorts, chewing a matchstick with which he picked his teeth.

In a dilapidated bure outside the shop, Rambaran's attractive daughter-in-law was in her customary hammock singing mournfully a song from Barsaat. Bhairo's deaf-mute son was sitting in front devouring her with his gaze. Now and then Bimla would throw a mischievous glance at him, seductively fluttering her eyelids. In response, his toothless grin would stretch from ear to ear revealing spittle at the corner of his mouth.

From somewhere inside the shop, Rambaran's wife whispered reproachfully, "Dulahin!" And Bimla straightened her orhini slowly and deliberately over her ample bosom, studiously avoiding her mother-in-law's eyes.

Dhanpat was distressed. He climbed down the veranda and took the path toward the swamp. At the swamp, Bansi was peeling pandanus leaves under a tree.

The swamp had swallowed several animals and children when it was wet and soggy. Mangal's eldest son had buried himself alive here twenty years ago. Now the swamp was dry; it carried only pandanus trees. And cattle and goats searched all day for anything edible.

Dhanpat waited for Bihari on a crooked wooden bench outside the schoolroom. Bihari was inside, prowling behind rows of exceptionally silent learners, hoping to catch someone talking. There was a loud clamor when the bell rang. Bihari dismissed his class and came straight to Dhanpat.

He had a letter for Dhanpat. Dhanpat limped along with Bihari, across a parched playground strewn with lunch wrappings, as the schoolmaster translated the letter, his reading punctuated by a regular asthmatic wheeze. Bihari prided himself upon his knowledge of Hindi and English and his ability to translate from both languages. He glowed in his superior knowledge as he explained every nuance, every shade of meaning in Somu's letter.

The letter was sad. It was unlike those letters Somu wrote from New Zealand. Those early letters mainly described landscapes and expressed bewilderment at the complexity of social life. They were enthusiastic letters.

Dhanpat didn't hear from Somu for a long time after he stowed away to Australia. However, he received reports of his levity with women and money, and the frequent bouts of depression he suffered. Rambaran once spread the story that Somu was in a mental hospital in India.

Dhanpat was alarmed; he worried about his son. Now, more than ever, when he heard so regularly from him. This was strange. He never had much affection for Somu. He wasn't like Dhaniram who went through all stages of life like a true Hindu. Dhanpat could trust Dhaniram. But his younger son invited only suspicions; he was far too restless, discontented, and given to secret thoughts.

The villagers regarded Somu as special. He didn't go to Bihari's school; instead he was taken into a mission school in town. They shook their heads in amazement and disbelief when he talked about books and ideas. This attitude changed to perplexity when he abruptly left his father. Finally, they were comforted in their initial belief that Somu was always a renegade.

Dhanpat saw quite early that Somu refused to be absorbed in the life of the village. These letters from Somu told more than he ever expected to know about his son. They were not addressed to him; it was always Somu talking to himself. At times he had wished that he would come back. Life would change; it would become whole and fine again for both of them.

Somu, of course, didn't return. But in a curious way Dhanpat's life was changing. There were words in the letters which echoed, and arguments which festered in his mind. It seemed that some unknown force had confronted him with truths he had hidden from himself.

His world was becoming rapidly disoriented. Things didn't seem to regroup again. His days oscillated between a past order and new anguish. At times he felt his life hovering at the edge of new perceptions.

There was, however, a loneliness now which was intense and complete. Was it because he feared desolation that he wanted Somu back?

The pale amber of receding sunlight rested on the distant Makai Hills and on top of tired and empty trees. It sharpened the grim profiles of the lugubrious huts.

The village was stirring again; the men were back from the fields and the mill. Dhanpat was at his prayer house under the tamarind tree. The door was open and the mixed smell of camphor and sandalwood paste was sharp and, to Dhanpat, reassuring. But when he confronted the icons and the brass idols, the momentary exhilaration, like a sudden inspiration, was followed by corresponding hopelessness. The gods looked old and ravaged.

He heard someone stir behind him. It was Bhairo.

"Arè, Arè, Dhanpat, you carry on. Don't worry about me," he protested, gesticulating.

Dhanpat placed the lota he was carrying at the door, and turned toward Bhairo.

They sat on the ground in front of the prayer house, and talked in low whispers. When Bhairo had left, Dhanpat sat there for a long time feeling old and withered.

This drought had laid so many old people in their graves, among them some of his closest acquaintences from the indenture days. Now it was Kanga's turn. How was he, thought Dhanpat, to regard all these deaths as quirks of fate?

Dhanpat had always considered himself inviolate. That was why he moved through life with such splendid reassurance. Now, sitting in front of the temple, he saw how the protective armor had gradually disintegrated. The tenuous bond that existed among the disparate items of his daily life was breaking. More than ever he felt the pointlessness of daily rituals of toil and rest, prayer and persistence. Once they were, however, the only affirmations of his existence.

He felt oddly defeated and humiliated. Dhanpat hurried into his hut like one excited over an unknown thing or one expecting an eruption. He fretfully closed the doors and windows and crept on to his string bed, and lay there in a delirium, his energies completely drained.

That night there was more looting and stone-throwing in the neighboring village. More sugar cane was burned.

It was Bimla's husband who, creeping and crawling home after a rum party, noticed the fire in Dhanpat's hut. He dragged himself from hut to hut yelling for help.

The villagers came with their machetes and cane knives, and with whatever water they could spare. They broke down the door with their machetes and pulled Dhanpat out of the blaze.

The dry and brittle thatch and bamboo crackled, wilted, then flared into flames, and were soon reduced to cinders. The rafters and poles also came down with an explosion, and burned on the ground, giving off a pale glow.

A moment ago there was total hush. Now the village broke into a tumult and then pandemonium.

Dhanpat sat silently amid wailing, shrieking women and children. Someone had thrown an old blanket around him. A couple of urchins crept close to him and stared, their faces revealing a mixture of fear and mute incomprehension.

Bhairo searched hard for any indication of guilt or shame on his face.

There was no sign of stress; he was stoic and inscrutable like the gods in the prayer house.

Dulari consoled her father in a low and husky voice, blowing her nose, and wiping her tears with the corner of her orhini. She helped him to his feet and directed him toward her hut.

Dhanpat felt something cold and damp on his thighs and down his legs. He examined his dhoti; he was wet.

In the weeks that followed, Dhanpat's insanity was argued and disputed. Then those outrageous stories began circulating. Bimla complained that she found Dhanpat peeping into her bath shed. Henceforth, the women moved in pairs or groups, and avoided him at the village well.

Bansi's son reported to his mother that the old man tried to molest him at the marshes. As a result, the children refused to walk through the marshes to school. And Bimla's husband said that one night, when he was sloughing back after a rum party, he met Dhanpat, apparently sleepwalking; he was stark naked.

Other stories were equally scandalous. Finally, the village elders met at the mandali and proclaimed Dhanpat an imbecile. They declared he was bent on inviting the wrath of the gods on the entire village.

Dulari wept with shame. Her husband was embarrassed. One morning, instead of going to the fields, he left for town. When he came back late in the evening, he was angry and disappointed.

The following day he took a village elder with him. Weeks later a government van halted in the village amid great shouting and clamor.

Dhanpat was taken away for observation. And the chief took possession of his land.

Tell Me Where the Train Goes

No. 3 skirted the foothills of Vunika and signaled its arrival with a loud roar. It thundered across the Vulovi bridge, the rumble growing louder and louder, and then groaned and hissed and came to a gradual halt with much collision and clanging of chains and metal. After disengaging the cane trucks the train chuffed off again to its garage.

Manu waited for the barking of dogs and the familiar splashing of water from a bucket. The barracks precinct was strewn with dog dirt; it would be difficult to avoid though his father carried a lantern.

The paraffin lamp glowed dimly casting wraith-like shadows which trembled and moved in the corner where Kunti slept. He clutched the old army blanket and curled himself inside. The floor was hard on his back. For a long while he listened to the whispers coming from the adjoining room through the wire mesh which was the upper end of the separating wall. Usually, toward midnight, talking died down in the barracks; after that all one heard was a chorus of snoring grunts. Manu felt terribly lonesome and afraid. Twelve o'clock was the hour of the earthbound spirits (there were whispers of Tevoro in the lines). But more than these, he feared the villainy of men from the barracks.

The nights were fraught with danger. Even in the moonlit night there were threatening whispers in the rustle of coconut fronds and mango branches. Sometimes he experienced a sense of foreboding at noon on a hot day when there wasn't a breath of fresh air, and the fields waited for some sort of strange eruption.

A rat chased some geckos across the cooking utensils. Manu felt a sudden chill run through his body; he uttered a hurried prayer, his gaze fixed on the quizzical expression on the countenance of exiled Rama. He was thankful for that picture which Jagannath had torn out of a calendar and pasted on the wall for him.

Almost imperceptibly the room was filled with an oppressive gloom; the oil was spent and the wick had burned itself out. He felt stifled by the mixed odor of kerosene and stale food. There was no ventilation; the only door had to be barricaded every night. He shifted close to the small opening in the wall which brought the draft in: the smell of dog dirt and urine was strong and nauseating. Except for the monotonous hum of mosquitos the night was still. He peered through the crevice. Fear surged in his breast. He held his breath and looked intently: in the dark something sparkled like a firefly. Someone was smoking a bidi cigarette which glowed and receded, glowed and receded. At that moment, Tipo gave a yelp of fright, fled to a safe distance, and growled. A whispering argument followed, and then a soft scurry of bare feet in the grass. Manu endeavored to turn around and face his mother but he dared not move: he was paralyzed with fear. His heart pounded frantically, he rallied all his strength and threw off the blanket and whirled around. Kunti was kneeling in a corner, sobbing.

In the morning, his father's body was discovered in the canefield. The women came out of their barracks, huddled together around Kunti, and wept. Kunti clenched her teeth and tore her hair, beating her forehead and breaking her jewelry: it was the final display of frenzied emotions. After that, her sensibilities dried up again and she collapsed in a corner. Manu never saw her so emotional again.

In the simmering heat of the noonday, they took his father's body on a bamboo rack and buried him on Kanacagi Hills.

A restless and sickly wind blew across the barracks in the evenings. The land was parched and many laborers stayed in bed with influenza. Manu watched the bats flitter in the dusk. He startled the flies which thronged the gutter in front of a detached shack where Kunti prepared a meal of rice and dhal and eggplant. She coughed and blew her nose, her eyes hurting in the smoke. Nowadays she seldom spoke. She answered curtly in a muffled voice when spoken to and then subsided in silence. Whenever someone called, she slinked quietly into the barrack. Now, more than ever, he wanted her to be open and confiding; instead she was self-effacing and secretive. He felt sadly unsupported and unclaimed.

After cleaning the dishes, she took the lantern from the kitchen into the barrack, and then barricaded the door. She made her bed quietly and sat despondently in a corner before falling off to sleep. Sometimes it frightened him the way she stared. She would gaze at him, her eyes abstracted, with such terrible intensity that he would want to run away from her.

Manu pulled the blanket over him and listened to the bats circling the mango trees and swooping from branch to branch, chattering and fighting, and gorging on ripe mangoes. He had seen Dhanai, pigmy-sized and misshapen, installed on a log in front of his barrack. Every evening he was there talking to Lakhan and Nekram and sharpening his cutlass. Manu noticed that Nanka no longer sought their company. This was not wholly surprising: here loyalties were transferred like changing of one's dhoti. And new allegiances were made without much remorse.

What these men discussed he didn't know but he was certain because of their sinister attention that in some horrible and insidious way they intended bringing harm upon him and Kunti. That evening, seeing him at the kitchen door, Dhanai grinned roguishly, baring his yellow fangs, and beckoned. Manu winced. Meanwhile Lakhan was scrutinizing him with his head tilted and his eyes screwed on him: he seemed completely oblivious to what Manu had seen at the pond. Both these men inspired fear and revulsion. He was particularly frightened when Dhanai hopped about the barracks with the stump of his leg concealed under his dhoti.

There was a piercing cry from the adjoining room followed by wild exchanges of profanity and loud sobbing. Lakhan was beating his wife again. Ambika sulked and cursed her fortune and gradually worked herself into a frenzy. "It's the engine driver's wife you want. Go to her then. She eat you like she eat her husband," she shrieked. Lakhan's large and powerful hand came heavily upon her back and Ambika's sobs dried up into snivelling hiccups.

How Manu wanted to escape this nightmarish world where life seemed continually menaced! He hated the sugar cane (Jagannath said it was Karkotaka, one of the main serpents of the underworld) and grieved for the youths who were prematurely shunted into the fields together with the ragged laborers. His refuge was the cave. When the barracks were empty, he would saunter through thickets and reeds to the cave with Tipo leading the way. The dog would give a shrill yelp and rush into the guava shrubs wagging his tail and forking his tongue in and out of his mouth. It was in this jungle he encountered the Fijian coconut seller whose leg was swollen with elephantiasis. He emerged quietly from the bushes, pursed his lips, and ejaculated a loud explosive noise. Manu almost panicked. Later they laughed together.

The cave was on the other side of Kanacagi Hills. Jagannath discovered it when they were collecting firewood. "It is Kailas," his father said. "The home of Shiva." It was bowed and lined like the head of a gigantic cobra in repose. Once he dreamed that its mouth closed and he was sucked through a dark tunnel into a pool which glowed golden and orange in the sunset. He was afraid when he returned the following day but it was safer here than in the barracks. Besides, he had Tipo. Here he rested, slept, and allowed his untutored but precocious mind to wander. He surrendered himself to images and echoes, hoping they would fall into a pattern.

Sometimes, after a night of turbulent wind and rain, he would walk along the gullies where the grass had been twisted and combed by the overflowing water. From the cave he would follow the drift of fleecy clouds on the wet hills and wonder where the train went. He longed to find out if the "mulk" that his father discussed with his friends was anywhere near the country where Mr. Pepper's memsahib had gone with her children. Inevitably he would reflect upon the secret his father told him about Yama, his half-brother.

If life was restful and orderly in the cave, in the lines it was forever anarchic. During the week, tempers frayed and quarrels broke out. Whether in the fields or in the barracks, the laborers' passions seemed totally unchecked by any instinct for self-preservation. On Sunday they were calmer. One by one they emerged from their hovels clad in their dhotis and squatted on their haunches in the hot sun. Kasiram tinkered with his harmonium for the most part of the morning and when everyone had lost interest he sang his favorite bhajan. Others smoked bidi cigarettes and chattered while Ramsamujh, the barber, made his rounds with a small tin suitcase, the scowl on his face becoming graver and graver as he moved from one head to another.

These were the refugees from a depressed sub-continent, gnarled and weather-beaten, and brutalized by ghetto life. Some had accepted their half-slave status, and a few seemed either bored or secretly dreaming of self-annihilation. There were others like Dhanai who were filled with destructive rage.

Almost unexpectedly the uneasy stillness was ended when Kunti, her face veiled by her orhini, shuffled to the water pipe with her bucket. Nekram nudged Dhanai, and Dhanai's small rheumy eyes shot up in flames. Manu had observed that whenever Kunti passed there were catcalls from Nekram and Khelawan, and the women wrinkled up their noses insolently or gave disdainful sidelong glances. Ambika was already at the pipe and a quarrel ensued. Although Ambika was as ugly as she was sullen and no one really cared for her company, least of all Lakhan, the other women came out on her side, and Sukhdaiyya and Padma actively aligned themselves with her. Ambika heaved incestuous abuse on Kunti. Kunti at first made shrill bursts of protest and then, to mitigate the humiliation, became loud and assertive. The men intervened when Sukhdaiyya grabbed Kunti's hair and threatened to put the chamarin's tail on fire by thrusting red chilies up her rectum.

At the end of these meanderings Manu felt hopelessly violated and betrayed.

The dogs began to bark again under the mango trees. Kunti was already up, her eyes fixed on Jagannath's cane knife. For weeks they slept in snatches and woke up when the roosters began crowing. One morning Kunti found a ball of feathers—a dead minah—at the door. Another time it was Tipo. There was a deep wound gouged on his back; it opened like an ugly and festering mouth.

The garandilla bushes were filled with the warm fragrance of ripe fruits and garandilla flowers. Lacking his friend's energy and feel for adventure (Kalika had evaded the fields for two consecutive days), Manu rested under the canopy of a rain tree overgrown with lianas and luxuriant garandilla vines while Kalika scampered, his curiosity flickering, from bush to bush collecting and discarding ripe fruits.

This was the closest Manu had come to the bungalow. From here the swooping curves of Kanacagi Hills, the sugar cane which resembled a series of playing fields, and the breathtaking green of the golf course provided an incredible vista. The lines were twenty-odd rusty corrugated iron and timber hutments, a physical and spiritual ghetto, huddled together at the bottom of the hills.

Manu followed the way Kalika had entered the bushes. He was nowhere to be found. He searched through creepers and clumps of elephant grass and, before he realized it, he was halfway into the summer house. The light here was made green by the lush growth of coral vines which clambered the bamboo walls, and tree ferns and wax vine growing in earthen pots. The lawn was freshly cut and trimmed. It was cluttered with frangipani and acadia trees which shaded plots of anthurium lilies and ornamental begonias. The damp smell of earth and grass and the intoxicating odor of frangipani lingered everywhere.

Everything about the bungalow was large: a massive hall and an enormous veranda decked with giant wicker chairs. In the kitchen the furniture and the pots and pans and the cutlery looked as if they had never been used. It was hard to believe, looking through the wire gauze in the windows which revealed rooms, one as spacious as the other, that these housed real people.

The entire bungalow was wrapped in a heavy brooding silence. At the end-room which faced a gravel path shaded by a giant fig tree, he stopped almost instinctively and prostrated himself on the flower bed. His heart pounding against his ribs, he summoned what little courage he possessed and crept close to the window. There was someone inside in his underwear sprawled on an unmade bed. It was the Sahib. He had a cigarette perched on his lower lip from which he took occasional puffs while he gazed emptily at the wooden ceiling. Without his khaki tunic and topee, his sunburned body looked small and vulnerable. It was certainly not the Sahib who ran his truck over Dhanai's leg when the latter was resting in a mill garage after lunch. Manu recalled with awe how the laborers cringed and stood in disarray, like frightened minah birds, when Mr. Pepper visited the barracks.

Manu was startled by a soft rustle of skirt behind him: a figure was moving through the hibiscus hedge, and then disappeared down the hill. He forced himself from the ground and followed her through the hidden pathway. He recognized her from the back: it was Kunti. Why wasn't she in the fields? What was she doing in the bungalow? He caught up with her at the pond. He hid behind some guava shrubs and watched. She loosened the knot of her long skirt and it fell on the ground around her. She stepped lithely over the tiny heap. Her hands moved to her small bodice. Naked, she looked taller than most women in the lines. She had a well-proportioned figure and Manu noticed how attractive her face was in spite of the mournful expression. In those parts of her body where the sun hadn't touched she was golden brown; the rest was heavily tanned. She freed the braid of black silky hair; it fell loosely down to her thighs.

Manu felt a mingling of curiosity, excitement, and guilt. He was entranced although he wanted to run away and hide himself with shame. He remembered his experience with Jumman's son when the latter tricked him into his barrack and exposed himself. There was a gentle tug in his own groin when Razak touched the ball of flesh nestled amid a tangle of hair. It had moved and become alive. He envied Razak's manhood and was ashamed of his small and shrunken body, and of pubes as bald as his skull which Ramsamujh had shaved after the funeral.

Kunti waded into the deeper end of the pond where strands of moss spread like clumps of hair, and the water was littered with brown and yellow guava leaves and petals of bush flower. Kunti took a deep breath and disappeared under the water. When she emerged from the pond, Manu had gone.

Throughout the week there was a brooding smoldering rage in the cane fields, the barracks, and even in the movement of trucks and engines. Early Thursday morning Jumman came running breathlessly to the lines to fetch Murgan, the sirdar. There was trouble at the weighbridge. Manu heard the report with morbid foreboding.

The dancers arrived on Saturday. In the evening, he saw Dhanai and Lakhan talking to the dancers. The dancers shuffled and turned on the red earth. They held their long skirts and glided, waving the silken scarves they carried in their hands. Now and then one of them would gyrate his groin provocatively and make little circles in front of the women. This brought roars of delight from the men, and the women pulled their orhinis over their faces to conceal their enjoyment. The drums thumped louder and the clink of anklets became more persistent. The faces of the dancers gleamed in the Coleman light. Someone from the spectators glided into the center and wriggled his hip amid wild cheering. The crowd clapped and swayed and shouted, "Wah wa! Wah wa!"

Dhanai and Lakhan were no longer in the crowd. Manu was alarmed by their furtive maneuvers. He searched for Kunti among the women. Sukdaiyya was rebuking Padma for displaying her pleasure too overtly. Manu asked Somari: Kunti wasn't there. He hurried back to the barracks. The barracks were empty; there wasn't a soul around. He followed the path leading to the pond. Someone was urinating under a mango tree. Further on, a band of men was clambering up the hill. With their lathis and cutlasses they could have been mistaken for a bunch of thugs. One of them carried a lantern which lighted their black, shiny legs. They were scurrying toward the bungalow. When they reached the garandilla vines they halted and crouched on the ground. Only Lakhan climbed to the bungalow.

Manu wiped the sweat on his forehead with his shirttail, caught his breath, and waited. He could hear the dull thump-thump of the drums, which was now indistinguishable from the beating of his own heart. Minutes later Lakhan returned, followed by a figure in white. The men moved closer. Only the one holding the lantern remained under the bush. The Sahib had barely reached the hibiscus hedge when they descended on him like a swarm of locusts. He uttered a loud agonized shriek, tried to retreat but stumbled and fell on the ground. "The motherfucker is drunk," someone cried, and kicked him in the stomach.

Manu gaped at this ritual of death and dissolution with muted panic. For the first time he noticed that the men were completely naked. Soon they were joined by a group of women who emerged from the bushes. They lifted their clothes and took their turns urinating on the wriggling figure who was pinned roughly on the ground by several pairs of rugged hands. A feeling of nausea was welling up: for a second, Manu thought he was going to be sick.

He struggled through thickets and elephant grass and threw himself headlong down the slope. In his mind he could see the men scramble to the pond to wash themselves. Then they would come for Kunti. He continued running, gasping for breath and throwing sidelong glances. He must find Murgan at the weighbridge. He came to a panting halt at the bottom of the hill but was spurred on by the thought that he was being followed. When he reached the mill precincts he was thoroughly bruised and scratched.

Manu heard No. 3 rumble over the bridge. He ran along the railway track leaping from plank to plank. He was reassured by the smell of molasses and coal, by the mill lights and the crushers which moved furiously. No. 3 drew closer and closer. He could see the fire box glow and throw sparks through the funnel like an angry monster. The train disappeared behind rows of cane trucks already waiting to be crushed. He must race past No. 3 and cross the tramline. If he waited it would be too late. He made a move, crossed the first track, and then faltered and tripped. Next instant he received a violent jolt and was thrown over the tramline into a heap of charcoal.

"We'll go away," Kunti was saying. He could barely hear her. All night he drifted into waves of oblivion. Now the throbbing ache in the back of his head was becoming an agony. Afraid that he would sink again, he forced himself to create patterns in the ceiling which was stained and splotched with smoke and dust. "We'll ask for land and go," she reiterated. This time he turned his face toward her. He knew she was lying. There was nowhere to go. They were simply shipwrecked in the barracks. Nevertheless there was a dim consoling hope in her voice. He noted that the old anguish had vanished from her face as if something had snapped free. She squatted beside him, her hand caressing his forehead. It seemed to him for a moment that once again her life was entirely for his preservation.

He felt strangely exhilarated and safe.

Groundlings

There was already a small crowd in the Regal's lobby. Mostly women from the shantytowns wrapped demurely in orange and mauve saris. And schoolgirls skirted, bloused, dimpled as in a recent teenage extravaganza, and reeking of talc.

The Gujerati ticket vendor regarded them truculently from inside his cage.

Having been warned of the groundlings we arrived forty minutes before the performance. We lingered in the lobby chewing peanuts and gazing at the stills of voluptuous starlets in a variety of melancholic poses. When the crowd closed in we jostled for position. In the struggle we were pressed further away from the entrance watched by two burly bouncers. Every now and then one of them stepped level with the crowd, rendered a massive jolt, and disappeared behind the sinister curtain while his mate stared at us, his eyes glinting with morbid hostility.

We rocked in swirling eddies, drenched in sweltering perspiration.

Our position was usurped by the schoolgirls; they giggled, mischievously giving us sidelong glances. We looked back in desperation: the sea of perspiring faces extended to the pavement. There was no way out.

It was then I spotted Mrs. Gupta, squat and fair, a large vermillion dot decorating her forehead. She was leading a brood of shantytown women. Apparently surprised to see us, she hesitated and then waved. We reciprocated with great alacrity, looking helplessly in her direction.

Mrs. Gupta carried her grandchild, and Chaaya, her belly swollen with her fourth indiscretion, was frantically bridling in her other children. Mrs. Gupta beckoned, indicating a small opening in front. We struggled savagely toward it while Mrs. Gupta, clutching the baby in her right arm, swung her left elbow once, twice, and we forced ourselves into the opening.

The two P.M. matinee was over. We surged forward in a wild stampede, compelling the mob cascading down the stairs to flee through whatever exit they could find. The bouncers snarled as we slipped and stumbled over each other, knocking ourselves against seats and outstretched legs, groping for empty stalls. Mrs. Gupta grabbed my wrist and hurled me into the middle of a row of vacant seats.

When we had settled in our stalls, she grinned, fanning herself vigorously with the end of her sari. The makeup on her face had cracked, revealing thin sprouts of hair on her upper lip.

We had lost Chaaya. The baby, still bundled in a woolen shawl, lay on Mrs. Gupta's lap. "My nati," she intimated, beaming inwardly. Dutifully I caressed the baby's cheek; it clucked and gurgled happily. Before I could object, the baby was on my lap. "Wait," cried Mrs. Gupta, waddling into the crowded aisle.

The circle was filling slowly. They came in pairs: men oiled and groomed, and women bejewelled and resplendent in glittering red and turquoise saris. We gazed from below: the men steered their wives to the waiting seats, fussed briefly (the women not wanting their husbands to sit beside other women), switched positions and settled down to watch the advertisements.

The creature on my lap was becoming increasingly petulant. It gave a prodigious yawn, scratched its nose, and bawled. I rocked my knees, tickled its ear, and hummed a ditty. The schoolgirls, who had found seats in front, looked back and tittered.

I felt something sticky sliding down my pants: the wretched thing was unloading God knows what! It continued to blare. Women who were cuddling babies looked, and sent sympathetic nods. In harassment I whirled around with the baby. Fortunately, Mrs. Gupta was shuffling down the aisle with bags of beans and a bottle for the baby. She swooped on the screaming creature (dropping the beans on my lap), fondling it and crooning strange endearments.

Soon the shanties and the baby were all forgotten. We were consorting with stars. Shrouded in darkness, we watched the screen lit up by the magic lantern.

The girl is dancing in the rain. Nubile and seductive, she is waiting to slide into her lover's arms in a most un-Hindulike fashion. We urge him on, and when he retreats we deride him. Her clothes are soaked, so that her breasts are thoroughly accentuated. No longer restrained by the contradictory impulses of modesty and excess, she pouts, placing her hands on her waistband, and wriggles her behind—for us.

We become loud and unmanageable. Heads begin to rock and swivel amid incessant shushing and tut-tutting. We crane our necks awkwardly. The bouncers stir again, flashing their torches on our excited faces, restoring order.

In the circle, men and their wives sit coldly in their seats as if bound to their congenital guilts. Only occasionally does one hear a slight flutter and an uneasy cough.

The protagonists are building a house. And they are singing of the price of rice and oil. Inflation! The advertisements had promised poverty and hardship. But there is little to disturb us from our inchoate dreams. Inflation is merely a song and poverty only stirs a bittersweet feeling, a soft ache. The house is totemic; concrete, steel, and ugly scaffolding are meant to lend verisimilitude. Then there is our court jester to save us from unnecessary anguish. He is a bellicose Sikh. Each time he appears brandishing his cutlass we chortle at his oafish ways. Mrs. Gupta nudges me, slaps me on my thighs, and works herself into a galloping hiccup.

The melee signals a denouement. Almost magically the black marketeers are beaten into submission. The sacrificial victim is the rain girl, now sari-clad and plainly Hindu. She suffers immolation, dumb as a cow, to save the world; but all this is not simply a facile solution, relieving us of the burden of interpretation. For us it is a flight from a world which forever negates magnanimity, denies heroism. Here nobility stands a chance.

And so, linked through our cultural residue, we rediscover the ancient dieties: the disillusioned university student is our holy man in search of truth and spiritual beauty, and his betrothed is the cow-girl in quest of her Krishna. They satisfy the need for gods. I look at Mrs. Gupta. She is blowing her nose, in the post-cathartic state, quietly into her sari. The instinctual response of a sensibility debased by fantasy. Her nose flower glistens like a firefly in the dark.

We drove Mrs. Gupta to the shantytown. Her home, a tiny shack, patched together out of heterogeneous scraps of timber and wood, had come up suddenly like scores of other sluttish huts. One weekend we saw a pile of crate timber and flattened barrel sides, and the following week there was a scraggy hut. The hutment straggled up to the ridges of a barren creek.

From a shack the radio was whining a tediously melancholic Hindi tune. In the yard barefooted children in rags scampered after a paper ball.

In the half-light, the shacks looked primitive and sad, like abodes of human debris which had fallen by life's wayside.

The advertisements had said the show was "the real reality." Now it seemed so utterly irrelevant; we shouldn't have gone. But then, it's always the same feeling.

At the end of the week we were looking through the papers again. "Manoranjan," the ads said, "India's answer to 'Irma La Douce.' "

We booked "upstairs"!

Tropical Traumas

When I first saw them, they were raking the already combed beach for sea shells, their attire—natty straw hats and marine trinkets—proclaiming their official status.

At last they discovered a dilo. It was passed around for comments amid exclamations of great surprise, and then dropped gently into a beach bag.

Soon I lost them. A mini-bus stopped in the asphalted area with an overzealous tour group. Eager to test the elements, they descended upon the resort like plunderers, invading the beach, the swimming pool, and the bures. Soon they were whooping and yelling in the water like children.

After a short burst of activity and decline, the burgeoning industry was just discovering the locals. I had found refuge from Suva's foul weather and the neurosis of the civil service and my own deceitful existence. I needed time for reflection.

The room was unremarkable, cheap, and antiseptically clean. And I had the sea by my window. I was satisfied.

I saw them again at dinner. Miss Baines, bespectacled, her face like ruffled papyrus, looked awkward in her flowered Susie Wong tunic. Mrs. Seabrook, the taller and quieter of the two, had short blond hair which lent a silvery aura to her gentle face. From their accents I gathered they were Canadians.

The attractive redhead, Felicity, was a schoolteacher from Palmerston.

"The way they feed you on the plane! I say it's quite immoral..." Miss Baines chewed her steak with her two prominent teeth, and added as an after-thought, "... considering that millions go without food."

Mrs. Seabrook had visited Fiji before.

"They used to serve lovely rolls in baskets with butter and marmalade. Now only the bread and butter. It's all changed," she pondered and frowned, dabbing the corners of her mouth with her napkin.

"And those cold sandwiches at Winnipeg. Oh my!" exclaimed Miss Baines.

The electric fan was whirling noisily. She wiped the perspiration from her forehead. Turning to me she asked what I recommended for dinner.

I suggested the local crabs.

"Oh don't," cried Mrs. Seabrook, waving her head. "They're those things with ugly blotches we saw at the village."

She looked at me pitifully and attacked her eggs with fresh gusto.

Just as we ordered coffee, Pierre, a French-Canadian whom the ladies had met at Honolulu, joined our table. We lit our cigarettes and heard him describe his checkered journey from Nadi.

"It was crazy," he gesticulated, thumbing the lump of his nose. "The longest damn bus trip in my life. Kept stopping at those shabby villages. And inside they jabbered and jabbered," he continued in his brusque manner. "How those three eight-wheel trucks and the buses crawled up the hills! It was crazy. Crazy."

The Fijian weavers and carvers arrived before the sun in their lava-lava. The carvers resumed work on their canoe; the weavers brought out their displays, and settled with their voivoi.

Their activities attracted curio-seekers and photographers but no pupils. The illusion, however, had been created; they were content to be simply picturesque.

At precisely two P.M. daily, Miss Baines and Mrs. Seabrook paraded down the beach in their gaudy bikinis, conscious of the quivering pleats on their stomachs and the blue knots on their thighs and ankles, but overtly brimming with a feeling of well-being.

Today they stopped to admire the long brazen figure of an Indian girl sprawled on a beach towel. The sun had found a new devotee; she was keenly testing its magical powers. She fluttered like an injured minah when she saw me, picked up her towel, and rushed behind a green and white cottage.

"I feel like a wet rat," cried Miss Baines as she came out of the sea with water sliding down her flabby thighs.

Felicity was on a skiff with Meli. She shrieked hysterically each time she caught sight of the shoals; often they were only silvery scales of the waves.

"Tell me," asked Miss Baines, undoing the plastic cap to free her hair, "tell me why some Indian women wear saris while others don't?" I told her.

"Now, isn't that marvelous."

Mrs. Seabrook agreed, evidently grateful for the learning afforded by travel.

There was a band in the bar on Saturday night. Miss Baines and Mrs. Seabrook sipped martinis, perched on leather stools, and watched the dancers.

Felicity was talking to Meli who organized cruises to the atolls. She wore a low-cut evening gown which exposed most of her softly-rounded breasts. She was explaining in clipped monosyllables the virtues of abandoned ceremonies. Meli recognized the evils of materialism and nodded; when she became incomprehensible he gulped his beer, wiped the froth with the back of his large hand, and pursed his lips.

The contradictory emotions of playing the host, being apologetic, and the deep offense given by aliens who monopolized the luxuries of his land, cocooned by wealth, had fixed a singular expression of shamefacedness and contempt upon his burly countenance.

Miss Baines was waiting for the barman to be free.

"And how are you, George?" she asked, taking a pleasant delight in the barman's name.

The lanky Fijian grinned in his orange and white uniform.

"Do they look after you well, George?"

"Well, sort of, Ma'am," replied George, reluctantly, wiping the formica surface.

"What do you mean, George, don't they treat you right?" The martini was making Miss Baines giggle; she endeavored to feign seriousness.

Mrs. Seabrook studied George coldly with disarming intensity. He looked nervous and ineffectual.

The Indian girl, dancing with an Australian sporting a handlebar mustache, was frantically evading my eyes. Her bronze skin had gathered patches of dark tinge in the sun.

"Well, it depends," ventured George, looking gawky and ill at ease, "on who is your leader."

Miss Baines knitted her brows and turned to Mrs. Seabrook to ensure she was taking in what was elicited with such verbal dexterity. Mrs. Seabrook nodded discreetly, fingering her pearls.

Earlier in the evening I had seen them talking to Nathan at the reception desk. A quiet and sedentary man, Nathan made an unlikely manager of a holiday resort. He endured harassments by the Australian proprietors and poachers from the neighboring villages with stoic resignation, perpetually planning a holiday he knew he'd never take.

Pierre was at the pool table in white flannel slacks and bula shirt; he was thoroughly peeled and flaked.

His ebullient manner had won him friends. Each time he wriggled his hips at his favorite waiter, his face disfigured by his grin, the other waiters quivered convulsively, falling over themselves with trays of drinks.

I moved with my drink to Lister at an empty table.

"Do you know," he had a way of beginning without preliminaries, "that 99.8 percent of the people here are psychosomatics?"

He was studying the impact of tourism on the upper reaches of the Navua River. I had picked him up by the Trade Winds; he had looked like a Peace Corps recruit, thumbing a ride back to his customary school after a weekend of dope and the Dragon.

". . . running from the disorders of temperate wastelands. It's their sado-masochistic tendencies which drive the tourists to exploit and be exploited." He was shouting above the band and tourist banter.

At the next table an English girl was telling her parents, her eyes rolling with excitement, about the glider trials at the Country Club which reminded them of some place in the old country. The old man sighed, it was such a pity they had to cram Tonga and the Cooks into this one trip.

Lister was yelling again. "See that redhead over there? Do you know her? Try and lay your hand and she'll give you that crazy jazz about the primordial. Philosophy of the genitalia, if you ask me. Nothing short of communal encounter for her!"

The band was playing a Fijian rhythm. Felicity was dancing with her mouth in the shell of Meli's ear.

The English girl, suppressing a giggle, was drawing her parents' attention toward a haggard figure in soiled and tattered attire, withdrawn in a corner with a mug of beer in one hand and a piece of bread in the other. He dipped the bread in his beer and chewed hungrily while gazing at the entanglement of ropes, unfurled sails, and braided masts attached to the ceiling to create an illusory galleon.

After he had eaten, he calmly picked up his canvas bag, threw it over his shoulder like the ancient traveler, and ambled out.

By the time I wandered to the beach, the solitary figure had disappeared around a sandbar.

I stood in a sheltered recess on the beach where the lights from the cottages didn't illuminate the sand or the sea, and listened to the incessant lapping and splashing of the waves which ruffled the night air.

On Sunday Pierre announced with a reckless look that he was taking a bus to Suva.

The clouds hung low over the sea, and it rained desultorily. There was a rough wind on the beach which kept the guests indoors; they gazed at the warring waves through rain-flecked windows.

At lunch they rushed out of the cottages with the beating of the lali; having momentarily freed themselves of one clock they rapidly adjusted themselves to another.

Late in the afternoon they came out to watch a lugubrious rainbow arched over the atolls.

When Pierre returned at the end of the week his face looked mauled and bloated; there were ugly folds beneath his eyes.

He didn't like Suva. The merchants were too demanding and an urchin had forced a salusalu on his neck and demanded a dollar. He obviously hadn't learned the rules, didn't care for the game.

He complained of the bad roads and bumpy ride. And the carefree hedonists no longer showered smiles like blessings.

But worse things had befallen him. A shoeshine boy had snatched his camera, and after harassment by the police he recovered it, only to discover on his way back that it wasn't the same one.

He evidently needed an audience; he sought me out.

"God damn it!" he exclaimed, gesticulating wildly. "The place is thick with thieves."

He brooded over his mishaps; the more he reflected, the worse became his temperament. Finally he worked himself into a rage.

Then his thoughts began to take a peculiar turn.

"It never works, does it?" His French-Canadian accent became more pronounced. "This bringing together of peoples. Fijians, Indians."

He peered angrily, his eyes brimming with rancor.

"It's a lot of problem. Trouble. It only means trouble."

What was a personal hurt was gradually transforming itself into a political credo.

"What about Quebec?" I asked provocatively, insensitively.

"Yes, yes!" he cried. "It's all the same. Vancouver, Auckland. It only means trouble."

He sat on the beach with his radio, pulled out the antenna and the leather case and examined the tangled wires inside, engrossed like a child in his toy.

Now he was chagrined by bad weather and sandflies. And the facilities were not altogether beyond reproach; he became querulous.

At first it was an insidious whisper. At the end of the week the news of the assault in the caves was splashed sensationally on the front page of *The Sun*. In the corridors, behind the bars, the waiters discussed all the sordid details of the brutal orgy.

There was an air of subdued expectancy when a taxi pulled in to take away Felicity's luggage.

For the first time Nathan hurried about, in an atmosphere of constrained hysteria, with a martyred look on his face.

At dinner Pierre sat alone by the electric fan with a napkin forced under his collar. The ladies too were silent except for the soft tinkling of cutlery.

I do not know why I expected some gesture or word which would reveal understanding. Perhaps because the stillness was too oppressive and unsettling.

I turned to Mrs. Seabrook. She was taciturn, then whispered, "Well, I wouldn't have put it past them, would you?"

The sand and the smell of the waves were beginning to creep into my dreams; I thought it was time to leave.

The taxis were bringing in more travel-stained tourists, smelling of airplane cologne, expensive cigars, and whisky.

As my car hurtled toward Suva, I thought of the ancient traveler for whom each new country wasn't simply a retreat but a place where, welcomed for his loneliness and poverty, he suffered its distress. Restless, demon-driven, he moved on slightly altered, but the leaving was always a loss.

Was he real or simply an obscure yearning, a figment of a romantic imagination?

I also thought of Felicity, and her ineluctable fate.

No Man's Land

Mosese edged his way through the crowded aisle, shrinking away from contact with the passengers, but inevitably brushing against a perspiring arm or perfumed hair. The driver looked into the rearview mirror, shifted the gears, and before Mosese could install himself at the back, the bus slipped away from Raiwaqa Market. Mosese clutched the strap for support.

And, just as suddenly, the bus rattled to a halt to collect more passengers amid noisy protest from those already inside. The driver leaned sullenly on the steering wheel and watched them scrambling in, dodging the heaps of refuse in tattered coconut baskets and cardboard boxes. Some of it was strewn on the pavement by a ribby pariah dog who fretted about the mess yelping impatiently. The new passengers shoved and squeezed into the aisle.

Mosese felt irritated. He hated people crowding against him; it was like an affront. He looked out. Across the ragged lawn, on the second floor, the stout figure of his aunt was dusting a mattress she had left out on the balcony to dry. At the same time she screamed at the hordes of children who raced up and down the dingy stairs, and on the balconies, soiling the morning's wash on the lines.

Mosese observed how the skin of paint on the sidewalls of the buildings had withered or wrinkled to form ugly scabs. Nearer the ground the concrete was covered with a fungus-like growth, and smeared with mud. Once designed to create an urban village, the buildings had degenerated into squalid colonies, huddled and overcrowded, receiving the city's dispossessed as well as regular arrivals from the villages.

The wooden frame of the bus creaked as it moved. It slowed and swerved for the pedestrians at the shops. No sooner had it gathered speed than it stopped again for the workmen who shoveled gravel and marl into potholes. Everyone turned or stretched his neck and looked out of the bus window.

When Mosese had just come from the village, nearly seven years ago, he would race up the stairs, like those children, to gaze at the sea or the overlooking houses on the foothills of Raiwaqa. He would wake before dawn and sit on the balcony with his school texts: the white roofs of houses would be wet and shiny, and the moist trees and grasses ready to sparkle in the sun. Sometimes he would stroll down to Laucala Bay, when the outlines of the buildings were barely discernible, taking in the cold damp air which was becoming infused with the smells of the waking day. With the morning sea whirling somnolently, he would be reminded how much the sea, the land, and the vegetation were still a part of him.

In the village he slept in his father's bure by the door, which framed the coconut and fig trees along the coast. And every morning through the crisscross of their trunks, he saw the sheen of water glint in the first rays of the sun. The sides of the hills, still covered in mist, were illuminated suddenly, mysteriously. His spirit elated, he sauntered across the beach to where the water touched the shore.

He was almost nodding off to sleep on the strap. The scars on the sidewalls of the buildings opened like fissures, and the brickwork came crashing down like refuse from a truck at the city dump. The inhabitants crawled out of the rubble like insects. And he, Mosese, ordered buses to take them away to the villages.

The strap was beginning to hurt his palm. When the road became open, the bus sped away. He watched the ochre-colored houses with carports and gates slip by. Some of them had "Keep out" and "Beware of Dogs" signs, even though there were no dogs about. Further ahead there were heterogeneous sun-filled apartments on reinforced concrete piles. And more derelict-looking shops. Hidden behind the hibiscus and croton hedges were the colonial bungalows, subdued and disintegrating, whose worm-eaten shutters were always fastened. Sometimes, in the night, he saw a pale glow of light through the slits in the shutters and wondered who their inhabitants were and what they did.

The waxen green foliage in the valley on the right became radiant as the bus crawled uphill, offering fleeting glimpses of the squatters' shacks underneath. And downhill the bus moved impatiently behind a green discolored garbage lorry which joggled down the middle of the road. The passengers turned up their noses against the awful stench which emanated from the lorry, and complained noisily, showing apparent enjoyment in the activity. At Flagstaff the lorry swung off to the right. The bus gathered speed again.

The village elder shook his head incredulously, his dark face shining under the dim kerosene lamp, as he passed the kava bowl to Mosese's father, and said the boy was sure to lose his way in the maze of streets in the city. Indeed, Mosese was afraid of the city, and it remained unexplored until he met Kini at high school.

Kini despised studies and he gave up after a year. But he continued to come to Raiwaqa to talk to Mosese and play his ukulele. One night he said to him: "All this scratching and study, where does it lead you? Only get your head swell up. No good for work or women." Mosese didn't argue. He simply looked at his friend's disc-like face, with rounded nostrils, a scruffy beard, and a thick spring of hair on his skull which he combed upward like his Black heroes. When he laughed, baring tobacco-stained molars, his eyes narrowed into tiny slits. He carried himself in a swaggering manner.

Although a year older, Mosese was not as strong. He had a lean and tensed frame and sallow complexion. The hair on his face and body was sparsely grown. And he walked with a slight stoop.

Kini looked disappointed: he apparently wanted to talk. When he persisted, Mosese cried out: "*Tiko lo,* will you? *Kua ni va' welei au.*"

"*Sa vinaka!*" Kini continued to argue. "*Tukuna mada vei au, 'o cei e na via wilika na serekali kei na ka sega na betena 'o vakavola tiko oqori?* Man, if you wanna change anything join a trade union." Kini spoke with the knowledgeable air of a dockworker.

"Get off my chest," he said. "Let me do my work, will you?" Mosese pleaded, gathering his notes on the table.

"Okay. Okay. I ain't said nothing," Kini hunched up his shoulders and concentrated on his ukulele.

Mosese tried to work but he couldn't: Kini was singing softly, tapping his leg with pleasure. Then Mosese's uncle arrived with his two friends from the cooperatives. They drank kava, talked and played cards. When his uncle had taken enough kava he would want to dance with everyone in the house. Mosese tore up the paper he was writing on, picked up his faded leather jacket, and went out.

Friday, he drank beer with Kini at Toorak and when the hollow darkness of the city was lit up, they turned in and out of the streets and alleys, blinking against the headlights of moving traffic, and found their way into the dance halls. The street lights dithered in the cold as they walked back home in the early hours of the morning. Next day, after Kini was off from the wharf, they bought food from a Chinese grocer at

Flagstaff: brown bread, canned herring, onions, and soda water, and ate hungrily from the tin by the sea-wall, pleased with each other's company. The smell of the sea debris on the desolate coast and the rough wind enforced a kind of solitude. They explored the city again until the early hours of the morning. Kini was never late for Church the following morning.

One night they rescued a salusalu boy from a gutter in Toorak. He was lying there like a crushed toad with blood dribbling from his nose. They took him to Raiwaqa where they saw his face and hands were blotchy and his hair crinkly and almost white. As soon as he recovered, he asked for a roll. Petero drank bad whisky from a shop in Toorak and visited prostitutes. And he looked barely twelve.

The city was at the brink of dissolution, and no one understood the danger.

Mosese felt disappointed when the bus slowed down to pull in at the terminus: he was almost beginning to enjoy the journey. Another bus compact with over-jovial shoppers squeezed past the waiting crowd, whining a warning. Mosese threw his jacket over his shoulder and waited: there was a scramble toward the door. He had told himself he would see Emosi at the jail and then stop at the waterfront for Kini. He dismissed the plan and walked briskly away from the bus stand. The hawkers cried "Beans! Peanuts!" There was something painfully unpleasant about their mean clothes, their lean and hungry looks. Who could believe some of them operated flats and taxis . . .

The market overflowed with people and produce. Taxis honked their way through the throng toward their customary stand.

Above, the sun grew fierce with the threat of rain. Sweat began to break out on his back. His legs felt warm and moist inside Kini's Levis.

There was no sense of crisis in the city: streams of shoppers hurried in their Saturday clothes across the street, dazed by the stinging heat into the cool of the supermarkets. On the Nabukalou Bridge they gazed like sightseers at the sluggish water below.

He turned onto Cumming Street. The ramshackle street was exploding with Saturday morning din: the slow noisy movement of taxis and vans; the cacophony of radio and recorded music from duty-free shops; and the shrill chatter of the shoppers. There were more than the usual number of policemen on duty. Mosese felt a dull excitement stirring inside him.

He sauntered on the pavement catching odds and ends of conversation. The smells of the street-stale food on the stairway of the Cumming Street Restaurant and decomposing vegetables in the metal bin in front of the green grocer were starting to impose on his senses. He stopped in front of a duty-free shop. The display window was crammed with radios, cameras, and Fijian handicrafts. Inside, tourists in semi-beach clothes were bargaining with the boisterous shop attendants who gesticulated and shouted, competing with the multiplying noises outside. "Business grown through sheer discipline and unflagging effort," read a business history in *The Fiji Times*. Mosese laughed quietly, cynically.

He joined the pavement crowd again. The reality of the multi-colored variegated crowd became accentuated in his mind. Corpulent sari-clad farmers' wives hunting for cheap jewelry jostled with elderly men in shirt sleeves reeking of tobacco, and school-girls skirted, bloused, and carefree. There were also Fijian women armed with trinkets for tourists, and loiterers drifting toward their favorite haunts. It was so easy for him to lose himself in the crowd. Their sweaty shining faces floated exuberantly, and the animated legs, some draped, others bare, swerved or collided, and glided past him. He saw the crowd closing in on him.. His head began to spin. Everything slipped into fragments of textures, odors, and sounds without color or warmth like a speeding mis-focused strip of film. It was like the exhilaration of the speeding bus. His feet moved independently of his mind. For a moment he thought he was going to panic.

A goods van pulled slowly across the pavement. He suppressed a half-desire to kick the metal. He waited impatiently.

One night Aunt Unaisi was going to close the door on him and he would be adrift in the city like a pariah, like Petero. He was without a job and had practically no money. And he no longer felt at ease with his aunt: when he wanted to be left alone she hovered around him picking up socks and underwear or comic books from the floor, and sighing impatiently. What prevented this threat of eviction from becoming a reality was his uncle. It was almost magical how the embarrassments of the day somehow vanished during the evening in the kindly and reassuring presence of his uncle who instantly established a joking relationship with everyone. Even with strangers like Brian who came to drink kava, and spoke English with a deliberately Fijian accent . . .

He was roused from his thoughts by a group of Fijian youths, who staggered provocatively amid the shoppers, dragging their feet on the concrete pavement. There was a quiet brutality in their movement. They stopped in front of a duty-free shop. The shopkeeper was soliciting at the storefront: now and then he ran his fingers through his well-spruced black hair and shouted amiable greetings at acquaintances in the crowd, his shiny white shirt pulled tightly around his paunch.

The rest happened quickly. One of the youths in a battered looking greasy car-coat, with a broken front tooth, drew close to the shopkeeper. The others feigned indifference and peered at the handicrafts. The boy in the car-coat lifted his face and spat in the shopkeeper's face. The shopkeeper looked as if he had been struck. The shoppers looked with surprise and waited to help. Slowly he pulled out a crimson handkerchief while the youths scampered away, laughing and punching each other playfully.

Mosese looked back over his shoulder. The lout in the car-coat stopped to clean his sinuses on the street. The shopkeeper moved. But only to shoo away the loiterers who had crowded around him.

Mosese broke away from the shoppers and crossed the street into a Chinese cafe. A Fijian waitress in a green uniform and dirty white apron sleep-walked to his table. "Yes?" she asked, involuntarily parting her lipstick-coated mouth. A cheap perfume whirled around his table. He ordered coffee. She gave the order to a Chinese behind the counter, who waddled off toward the kitchen in shorts and sweat-stained singlet.

When they mentioned fencing at the meeting, he thought of Bechan: the diminutive figure of the old man crouched on his haunches, pulling out muraina weeds with his two calloused and bony hands. The sun was unusually savage here, and Bechan's only protection was a piece of rag on his skull. It was futile labor: by the time he had cleaned half the paddy the young rice was quickly overtaken by the stubborn weed.

When the sun began to smite his shriveled-up body, he took his cattle to the nearby creek, and drank from the cup of his hand. He sat under the scant shade of a charred mango tree, chewed his roti, and watched the cattle pulling at parched ropes of paragrass from the edge of the paddy.

Mosese saw Dhania, Bechan's wife, daily prancing about the dirt yard around their weathered shack, which stood bleakly in the landscape like an aberration. She would be sweeping the yard or hoeing her vegetable garden. On Fridays, she plastered the floor and walls of the hut with a thick sludge of mud mixed with fresh cow dung, and sprinkled cow dung mixture in the yard. Her long blue skirt trailed behind her in the slush.

Once Mosese brought her some dalo stems. She offered him roti and eggplant curry.

The waitress placed the coffee on the table with a clatter, spilling some of it on the saucer. The coffee was strong and frothy at the edges with a film in the middle. He sipped slowly, savoring the coat of milk against his palate. Gradually he lost the feeling of tension.

He thought about the meeting again. He had gone almost against his will. Kini said it was clandestine to heighten the sense of drama. A single light bulb hung from the blackened ceiling and lit up what looked like a dilapidated church. Kini tramped on the dusty floorboards, shaking hands and directing people to the benches, like one who had the situation thoroughly well in hand.

That was what gave Mosese confidence—the nonchalant way in which Kini moved. There was a lot of laughter and talking and speeches. Most of the time Mosese gazed out of the window at the squatters' huts in the mangroves by the waterfront, until someone spoke of Idi Amin and people around him stood up and applauded.

Back at Raiwaqa he told Kini how difficult it was to arrive at a position in which to reflect when no one understood who was staying and who was going. At least one ought to know the owner before he could think of burning the house down. In reality he was afraid of starting something which in the end no one would be able to control.

Yet the present frenzy was inevitable, indeed necessary, for future wholeness when the land and its inhabitants will be returned to their original impulses. He agreed with Kini that the rural cause was the only wholesome and pure cause. Although like many others they had come to Suva to escape, for some time, the hardships of the soil, and now had made the transition and become captives of the city, still the rural cause was their cause. After all, as Kini said, it was the idea that mattered.

Again he had experienced the contradictory emotions, one hardening into something like faith, and the other bringing about doubt and despair. Kini looked at him impatiently and criticized him for a lack of spirit, "*E sega ni macala vei au na nomu i vakarau.*" And continued to thumb the pages of *The Sun*. They quarrelled when Kini brought up the subject of his Tongan blood. For the first time he felt truly vexed with Kini.

That night he went back to his notebooks. He worked far into the night. Nothing he wrote seemed to have truth: it was impossible to find the precise words for his feelings. He decided true things are never written down, like the village mekes, and the songs of creatures from the bush and the sea.

However, he felt inhibited and mangled like the lekas who inhabited his imagination. There were thousands of them in the bush; they squealed with laughter, and sometimes cried for home.

In the kitchen, the radio was loud; outside it was very still. His thoughts hovered on the fringes of sleep, and his head lolled to one side on the wooden chair.

It was raining in the bush. Mosese had gone with Jioji to fetch kerosene from the cooperative store. Kani sniffed about, as if she too were overpowered by the bo ni bogi, and darted from one clumpy thicket to another. It was she who discovered the two girls bathing in the pool.

The ground was soggy and covered with dead breadfruit leaves. Nearby, a ripe breadfruit had fallen, burst, and decomposed. A sour stickly smell pervaded the air. Anisa squirmed and giggled, swaying her rain-washed face from side to side under him. It was almost nightfall when he woke up to the sigh of rain and the flapping of pigeons.

He roused himself and looked up. The waitress was watching the changing emotions of his face. He noticed she wore rouge to conceal the Friday night's creases, and was transfixed in an odd position. "She's a bitch alright," he frowned and looked away. Like those girls Kini chases. They feel you up pretending they are touching you there, when all they want to know is whether you can afford the "Dragon," where they could disappear with someone like Brian.

He paid the waitress. The smell of the scent followed him to the pavement. A spasm of warm air brushed against his neck as he stepped out. He cleared his throat, coughed, and sucked out the mucus: it tasted like the film of milk in his coffee.

Now he moved with quick strides over the bridge. Excitement was welling up again. Any bodily contact with the shoppers was like a violation; he wanted to retaliate. He made angry little noises, and quickened his pace. Past Woolworth's, the car park, and the busy shopfronts, he was in the sun again.

There was a strained immobility in the knots of people along the arcade. Traffic police on motorcycles streaked past the parked cars, waving down the traffic; there were detour signs further up. Beyond the signs the road was open, and heat melted down on the simmering pools of black on the street surface.

There was no sign of tension. There was threat only in the broken rain clouds which scurried over the sun causing swift smoky shadows that slithered over Sukuna Park. Across the harbor, Lami was partially concealed in industrial smoke. There was more smoke in the distance, coiling upward from the villages deep inside the forest-clad hills.

Someone hollered his name: it was like a frightful explosion inside his head. He looked back and responded with a short nod of his head. Some of the marchers were visible around the bend. He was almost jogging now. Sweat was streaming behind his ears and down his neck. He stopped near a service station. Minutes ticked by. The marchers were moving past the Regal. In front of him was a station wagon, sky blue, glowing brilliantly in the sun.

The marchers drew nearer. Leading the march were elderly men in coats, sulus, and sandals. Their dark closely-shaven faces were expressionless. When they closed their somnolent eyes to blink away perspiration, the creased and puffy bags below their eyes quivered, and trickles of sweat raced down their cheeks like tears that have been squeezed out. They marched slowly and solemnly, gazing blankly ahead. Only the racial slogans on the placards were loud and angry and, in the context, incongruous and obscene.

Kini wore a black T-shirt and dungarees. He was among the younger men at the rear who showed a serious pleasure in the march. Someone cheered from the spectators; Kini brandished his placard clownishly at him and waved.

The few moments seemed timeless. The sight of the marchers became blurred and the hum of the crowd was muffled and faded into the background. Nothing impinged on his consciousness now except for the damp shirt which touched his back like a dull electric current. Something inside him snapped like an expanded cord. The excitement had abated. The crisis was over. He was overcome by a quiet exhaustion, like the feeling of disappointment and emptiness after a movie, when the fans are switched off and the exit doors are opened for the spectators.

His eyes had moistened with tears. The ache behind his head gathered like a rage ready to burst open. His right hand held a twenty-cent piece. He clenched and unclenched his fist. He felt the pressure of the crowd again on his back. He swung his arm with sudden violence and struck the blue station wagon twice and kicked. All eyes were riveted on the marchers who were turning toward the government buildings. No one saw him come out of his stupor, and disappear in the passing throng.

A Fijian, with somewhat balding head, in flowered bula shirt, came out of a take-away shop with several greasy parcels of food. As he approached the station wagon, he looked for a moment as if he were going to break down. He swore bitterly in Fijian, and crouched on the pavement, pushing the parcels awkwardly on the seat, and ran his fingers over the torn paint. He swore again, "Bastard! Bastard!"

Marigolds

I can hear the gurgle in the toilet, and water rushing to fill the cistern. In a moment the toilet door will unlatch. Dharma will be in the kitchen again. And I'm clinging hopelessly to this Sunday morning, afraid of the waves of depression that hit us about 2 P.M.

Throughout the night I dribbled copiously like a baby; in the morning, woke up with the dreadful sensation that my hair had turned crimson, and flesh dissolved into a vegetable curd. In spite of countless experiments with digestive habits, especially after they diagnosed a cancerous growth at the lower end of my alimentary canal, I still have those dreams. I must have struck the iron of the bed with my left arm. It flapped at my side like a broken wing as I limped to the balcony to warm my bones. Dharma, up earlier than usual, had slipped out in the dark for her Sunday ritual. My wife is a sun-worshipper. She pours cold tap water from a brass lota on a Tulsi plant as the sun rises, chanting some obscure Sanskrit mantra, which I'm sure she does not understand. She pulls the orhini over her head when she discovers I'm watching.

There used to be such a pleasant chirping of birds in the trees when we had just built the house. Now the bush is gone, leveled by squatters. Our house is a bit ungainly. Dharma was elated when it was finished. She has kept some marigold seeds in a bottle. She said she'll have a garden. We don't have a garden yet. Except the dried-up flower bed in front which carries Dharma's Tulsi plant.

The sun is a shimmering disc. I can feel it soaking up the moisture from the grass. Lord, the incurable distress of a vacant, bright Sunday! Each time there's a scrunch of wheels on the gravel, my attention is automatically drawn to the street, expecting to be rescued from this self-made prison. Dharma inevitably gravitates toward the kitchen. My fingers begin to twitch nervously on my lap as I wait for the prattling in the kitchen: it will fall like an avalanche down from the crevices of my head, tearing my nerves to shreds. I'm relieved she's standing in the middle of the kitchen, staring vacantly at the smoke-stained walls. She sighs ruefully. I watch her rouse herself and walk into the passage. She throws a quick evasive look into the lounge and slinks into the bedroom. I can picture her flexing the muscles of her toes, studying her fingernails or gazing emptily at the bare walls.

Last week my mother left our house. One morning, she flew up in a rage, accusing me of wanting her out of the way. She starting flinging everything I had given her at me: blankets, medicine, tobacco. She called a neighbor and had her things removed to the destitute home. I went to fetch her in a taxi after school. She refused to see me. "Mother," I pleaded, "I have come to take you home. Why are you playing these games? You know I want you back, Mother." For a second I thought she was going to scratch my face. "Aach!" she shrieked, trying to control herself, and turned away from me.

She'll come back. Out of spite. To humiliate me, accuse me of ingratitude, and taunt me with her craziness. She'll mutter away in Hindi: "My little nigger who wanted to fly. So she has clipped your wings. You are a disgrace like your father. Treating a poor, ailing woman who is your mother like this. . . . You can't treat me like this, you know! I will tell the magistrates. I will let the whole world know. . . . So Cheta is ashamed of his illiterate relatives because he is a big man with a post. . . . You are nothing, I tell you. Nothing." She'll spit her phlegm in a tin half-filled with red mud which she keeps by her bedside. When she is calmer, I'll listen to all her complaints about her ailments and give her tobacco money. Her limbs are crabbed and gnarled by rheumatism. She seldom sleeps when the night is cold. She sits in the dark smoking homemade cigars. Her skin has become dismal like the cigars she smokes.

As a rule, Dharma has absolute reverence for convention. However, she is most un-Hindu in her contempt for trespassers (trespassers destroy our equilibrium!). She despises my mother, above all, who she swears is a demented witch come to destroy our house. The old grimalkin pampers her in that belief. All day she plays strange tricks with Dharma, and laughs ghoulishly when the latter is not watching.

Sometimes I amble along to Mr. Rangaswamy's house. I can see the postal clerk squatted in a semi-lotus position on his porch, reading.

"Unclaimed trash filched from the Post Office," I quipped once to impress Dharma. Mr. Rangaswamy's two passions, his only weaknesses he claims, are yogic breathing and politics. He offers me the disemboweled car seat, mounted on a board and pushed against the wall, to sit on. I listen to his bleating South Indian voice, hoping to be affected by some of his enthusiasm, as he unearths the issues and hidden trends in government, and belches intermittently to emit stale, sour wind from his chest. The wisps of gray hair on the sides of his balding head quiver as he becomes increasingly eloquent. Abruptly he relapses into silence, nodding toward my house. "She has been on the balcony twice." And totter back, my brain inflamed. The lurking beast inside the cage of my ribs lifts its head like a pre-historic monster. Once in the lounge, however, all my rage is doused. Dharma, almost disappearing in the bedroom, waits for me to react, then skulks inside. More than anything else she resents the reproaches that I never make. Silence is my secret weapon.

There's an unhappy, sullen doll on my bookcase. Dharma bought it to decorate the lounge. Like my wife, she watches all my thoughts from some secret vantage point. One weekend I broke her head. I can see a film of tears in her glassy eyes.

After my visit to Mr. Rangaswamy one Sunday, I was slicing cucumber in the lounge. I shuffled into the kitchen for some salt. Dharma turned with a start, and cringed with fear when she saw the knife in my hand. She howled like a crazy woman, bolted outside, and hid behind a hedge. All afternoon there was a trapped, threatening air in the house. It was then I realized how our life had gradually slipped beyond the margin of security. She stole inside after dark, and locked herself in the bedroom.

Each time Cecil returns from Australia he seems darker, swarthier, older. The Australian climate doesn't seem to agree with him. He stays at our house during his brief vacation. He brings his daughters, two of the most secretive and unpleasant children I know, to show them the island of his birth. He rarely goes out even when the weather is fine. When he is tired of sitting in the lounge, he takes a mat behind the house and sprawls under the mango tree in his t-shirt and slacks. Tremors of brotherly love ooze from the depths of my flesh when I watch him lying there under the mango tree, waiting for a soft breeze. There are so many things I want to know and discuss. But Cecil has always been the quiet one. All I know about him is he's a dentist in Sydney, has two houses, and his wife Dorothea is a nurse.

The children, wrapped in coarse woolen clothes in spite of the stinging heat, are always in the passage, whispering in each other's ears and throwing furtive glances at us. They aren't like real children, soft and innocent, but unhealthy looking and adult-like in their demeanor. I tried to take the younger one in my arms. She wriggled out crying, "You smell like an old man!"

In the bathroom, I peeled off my clothes, and stood, naked, in front of the mirror and sniffed my body. Sure enough, the dried-up hide that encased my limbs emitted a fetid smell—the odor of death. I paced like a trapped animal in the lounge making loud shuffling noises until Mr. Rangaswamy came out on his porch, spectacle in hand, and peered quizzically at my behavior. I bought some lotion on the way home from school and splattered myself with the stuff. Dharma's cold, frowning eyes told me she didn't approve. She felt pleasantly tormented by the thought that she had somehow been betrayed. I hid the lotion in a cupboard.

Once again my attention turns to the diurnal sounds that signal the passing of hours: the change of radio music; the squatters chatting softly under the growing shadows of houses after their siesta; the children out in the yard with their kites. The air of torpor has slowly vanished. There's no longer the frightening noonday stillness which had invaded the huts. The kites glide like tiny machines against the glistening blue vault. Imperceptibly the afternoon, now a shade cooler, is wearing on. I have seen the wind steal behind the house; the leaves of the mango tree are astir. Dharma is urinating noisily: she has left the toilet door ajar.

At precisely 9 P.M. each night Dharma is in the bedroom, dusting the sheets and pillows, pulling down the mosquito net. By 9:30 she's in her clumsy nightwear on her side of the bed. From there she gauges my actions by the movement of my slippers. She knows exactly when I'm fumbling with the strings of my pajamas, turns briefly to see I'm settled in, then pulls the cord to switch the light off.

I toss and turn feeling for a soft, comfortable place on the pillow. With my eyes shut I muse about the marigolds, groping through a labyrinth which is now a crater, now a tomb, waiting for the deliriously happy state of being suddenly afloat. Abruptly, without much effort, without losing breath, I'm flung upward like a billowing parachute. I propel myself higher with my elbows—it's one skill I'm sure of—into a vast, open field of heavy-blowing marigolds. Acres of succulent plants, the size of sunflowers, blazing maddeningly in the sun, still straining for growth.

The latter part of the dream is less pleasurable, more threatening. The voices of children, forever on the fringe of audibility, lead me through a meandering pattern to the stone altar under a crumbling thatch, smelling of goat dumpings on the sides, where I suffer reproaches from the shadow. I do not know who I am or where I am. I squirt my eyes open. Then begins the agonizing effort to push myself afloat again. Slowly light walls up, and the familiar surrounding slides into place.

I brought a sprig of marigold for Dharma's hair: the stunted flower was glowing like a jewel in the school garden. She left it in the lounge. When she came back for it, I had taken the flower in my mouth.

For years I looked after the school garden. Until they made me the deputy head. Now I virtually run the school. And feel quietly superior. The head is an odious fellow, seen hurrying in the corridor, jangling a bunch of keys and giving everyone a formal nod like the previous head. He has an infuriating habit of peeking into the staff room and flicking his tongue between his lips that are burned by alcohol. He pretends he is seeking Mrs. Sharma for consultation. (Mrs. Sharma already looks peeved and ready to burst into his office.) Meanwhile, his snout is turned toward Hina. Hina tilts her face in query, and fumbles into her handbag for a handkerchief to blow her pretty nose. Her mouth opens in youthful laughter, as soon as he moves away, revealing all the slippery membranes inside. Yes, I have allowed my eyes to roll on their youthful limbs. But mainly for the pleasure of catching them in a coarse, unguarded gesture. Each morning for some obscure reason I expect a slight limp in their erect torsos. I had to pay dearly for my surreptitious action. I dropped behind Hina in the staff room one morning: she was hopelessly smothering a giggle at the mention of a wad of cotton wool to prevent the yellow discharge in my right ear. Since then she has taken instructions with averted eyes.

I haven't picked up any of the urban smartness. Still, I can see through all the blatherings and boastings in the staff room, all the desultory conversation about their precocious children who are studying medicine or law, their new-fangled houses (on stilts) in Beach Estate, and the relative performances of their shiny cars. Sufficient to drive anyone distraught! Most of them ignore me, behave as if I do not exist. I'm not game enough to be asked to their Friday night drinking parties. I have struck up a friendship with Eroni, the physical education instructor. The Fijian lad is the only person who takes me seriously, calls me "Mr. Chetram" politely, even though he regards me as a member of the desperate, money-grubbing fraternity which he despises but secretly hopes to emulate. He shakes his head at my frugal lunch, and smiles pitifully. Eroni affirms the historical basis of my existence.

It takes me a little longer each morning to dispel the clouds from my head and arrange my thoughts before I enter the classroom. The students no longer take seriously all the postures I assume for their benefit: my magnanimity, my cheerfulness, my warmth. Instead they ridicule my blustering ways, and snigger with a criminal leer on their faces when they find me in disarray. Encouraged, of course, by the blush of anger on my face when I grope for words or silence the amused chuckle in the back.

Standing alone in the staff room toilet in front of the gushing water in the bowl, after the Friday morning session, I saw clearly how my whole existence has been in bad faith. The lies I had lived in order to hold, to maintain serenity, accepting countless humiliations without rebelling, suppressing all aggression out of fear of creating new situations which I might not be able to control, where my tolerance was just a mask to preserve my inner freedom and weakness, my reticence an empty posture to cover my defects and avoid censure, had warped everything that was wholesome and fine in my life. Now the certainty on Dharma's face stabbed me like mockery.

I did not return wearily to 21 Yala Street that Friday afternoon with my statchel and umbrella. At noon I slipped away from the agitated staff and their provocative pupils toward Suva. All my life I had lived according to other people's expectations. Now I wanted a life of my own to start a new road. The passengers smiled strangely at me on the bus: I was the lost member of a tribe just returned to the fold. I strode in the swirling crowd on the pavement remembering the faces, odors, and cravings which had slowly been obscured in my memory. Again the city was the mela of my childhood where lost amid the tents, stalls, and games, I roamed like a free spirit. The splash of color were myriads of marigolds. The warm fragrance of the unseen flower suddenly pervaded the air. I waited for the sense to snap open.

Afterward the stalls, the tents, the games were all washed by rain.

I cannot distinguish, having become a prey to so many delusions, how much of what happened that night was real, how much simply a dream. I recall feeling that all the unlit streets and alleys, vacant rooms and parks were so many empty and unillumined realms of my existence. The boisterous, good-humored taxi driver steered me into a bar which smelled of urine and sweat. I told myself I shouldn't have taken so much alcohol. I detached myself from the drinkers and headed toward the toilet. The bowl overflowed on the greasy floor, and bits of newspaper and cigarette butts swirled in the pool of water. I waddled outside to clear my head.

The dingy metal cage inched upward from a subterranean depth. It seemed like a slow drift into the air from the labyrinth of my dream. I could have remained there all night but for the wiry creature in a hippie blouse who stared strangely at me, coughed nervously when our eyes met, and dropped his gaze involuntarily on the spent match which he rolled with his toe. When the gate slid open I broke into a run. He followed me to the pavement like a shadow in a dream.

The taxi driver surfaced again and lumbered along by my side. Like kindred spirits we marched into a restaurant. My companion ordered several Chinese dishes and beer. I watched him in the wall mirror, totally enthralled by the vigor of his conversation and his appetite, as he chomped his food in a ravenous fit. "Damn it," he cried, swigging from a bottle. "It's so easy to be happy. So damn easy." There were drunken tears in his eyes. His face gleamed with perspiration.

And then the drunken ride through the resisting darkness. The streets were washed by rain. The car stopped at the desolate end of the city. My companion shot out in the rain with his coat over his head, and disappeared into what looked like a run-down bungalow. I waited with spluttering desires; was relieved when there were no catcalls or jeers from the neighborhood. I trudged laboriously up the short flight of stairs, egged on by my companion, almost stumbling on a cat which purred persistently against my legs. My breath became loud and phlegmy. I felt a curious weakening of the knees. I must have been sick afterward. There was vomit in my shoes. The mattress smelled of child's urine.

Dharma didn't sniff me all over or taunt me with questions as she is wont to do. She sat on the sofa in her crumpled nightgown, brutally quiet. I ignored her and staggered into the bathroom. When I came out she was sobbing quietly, her head between her knees. "Stop it!" I cried, feeling anger welling inside my head. "Stop it this minute!" She looked up fiercely, trembled, and bawled. A light suddenly appeared on Mr. Rangaswamy's porch. I struck her across the mouth. She gulped and reeled back, emitting a stifled shriek. I clutched a braid of tangled hair and reached for her throat. She struggled, knocking the doll onto the floor. I struck the doll aside, and hit her again, and kicked her in the groin, and left her in a heap. I locked the bedroom door and crawled into bed.

The serenity has gone from the day. There is turmoil in the sky where heavy black clouds are lit up by wafts of red like blood. Our world is shrinking. There's a hopeless gulf between the lounge and the kitchen. After the futile gesture, my pathetic freedom, what was I to do? A slow anguish grips my heart, the anguish of being unsupported. Everything, history and customs, had prepared me for this impasse. There is no alternative life: a hundred years of history on these islands has resulted in wilderness and distress.

In a moment I'll shift to the balcony. The kites are fluttering in the eddies.

Dear Primitive

Elaine crossed the arcade with a vague sense of unease. Suva looked stale and sickly bright in the sun. How quickly the next morning, which began so cheerfully for her, had exhausted itself: burned itself out, she thought. She smiled weakly at a pupil in holiday clothes. At the crossing the shoppers merged and then broke into different directions.

She woke up rather early in the morning and sat on her bed, legs folded, and watched the light pour in through the diffused clouds. That old feeling of being bruised and imprisoned had disappeared. She told herself at last she was beginning to come to terms with herself. After a quick breakfast of eggs and cold milk, she took the bus to Suva, feeling a little guilty for this weekday freedom. But she managed to brush the feeling aside. Once in the city she did not know what to do. She sat through a movie with six other people in the entire cinema. Afterward she wandered absent-mindedly from shop to shop and bought things she did not require at Woolworth's. During the weekend there had been a tourist ship at the wharf and the streets were full of foreigners. Now the city looked empty. She walked to a Chinese restaurant to eat after the lunch-hour customers had gone. She sat there for a long time smoking and listening to the soft rattle of the bead curtain—like pebbles under water.

To avoid returning to her apartment immediately, she decided to stroll along the sea wall back to Nasese. She lived in the old section of Nasese, consisting mainly of wooden bungalows which were being gradually overtaken by new concrete houses on stilts. The bungalows had a permanently neglected and melancholy look: the paint had worn off from the wood, the galvanized iron roofs were rusted by the action of sea water, and weeds flourished in the back yards. The front wooden fences, festooned by insects, needed repair. Once the residences of European civil servants, the bungalows were now owned by Indian merchants from Suva. Elaine rented a semi-detached house here. It was cheap and near the sea.

She threw the windows open. The sea appeared choppy and the tide lapped against the sea wall, rocking the sea debris. She had planned to wash her hair but soon lost interest. She hitched her dress over her thighs and dropped on the unmade bed. A bee buzzed against the screen door, found its way into the kitchen, and continued to buzz among the dirty utensils. She heard the faint clank clank of a knife in the neighbor's garden which added sadness to the still monotony of the hot afternoon. She picked up a hand mirror from the mantle piece and studied the profile of her face and hair. Her face looked burned and puffy and her hair, yellow like corn, was plaited as in an old photograph taken when she was nine.

She often asked herself why she had stayed when all her old acquaintances had either left the islands or were planning to leave. The shop keeper at Nasese often asked her, "So, Miss, when you leaving?" Why did she stay? What was she waiting for? There were no easy answers to these questions. Her immediate response was she stayed because this is where she was born. This was her country. There was no where else she wanted to go. But her relationship with the country was vague. After her parents had settled in New Zealand and Ronnie left her abruptly that night, there seemed fewer links with the place. She knew the world around her would never open up to her completely. Yet she waited for it to open up and claim her.

Her relationship with Ronnie was based on a chance encounter: it finished with the suddenness of such a contact. Ronnie had come to Fiji with the express purpose of making the best of the sun and sea. This brief romance with a good-looking girl born in the islands completed the pleasure of a package tour. Every weekend he drove her to the holiday places and tried out the food and facilities at different resorts. She was of course grateful for his attention. She even tried to evoke within herself a sense of adventure for his sake. For a short period at least her past seemed like a dream that was over. However, all these activities in the sun left her feeling a little fraudulent, like pretending to be happy on a melancholy day. She realized that no amount of active life could thaw the cold spot that was in her past. It was there she wanted him to reach her and understand what it was like.

It wasn't long before she discovered that one world was shattering into another. It happened first at the golf course. Ronnie was crouched on the green, leaning forward, his left elbow on his knee, putter in his right hand. The greenskeeper was burning mounds of grass on the edge of the fairway. Suddenly the green started to smolder and crackle. She felt a wave of heat against her face. The sky turned orange, saffron-splashed. A heat mirage danced in front of her and pursued her across the green. She hurried back to the safety of the club house. From there she saw the grass was all consumed; there were two dark smoking patches where the mounds had been. Ronnie and the greenskeeper were transfixed where she had left them.

She asked Ronnie that night if he believed there were things about the islands which no outsider could ever understand. Her father used to say that about the sea and the hills at Vandrakula.

"But you aren't a foreigner, my dear primitive," Ronnie replied in a jocular manner.

"I know," she answered quickly without looking at him.

Ronnie stared at her face for a moment; then started to tell her about the tourist couple he met at the yacht club. She didn't want to pursue the subject any further.

Elaine worked with the children all day, and learned many ways to occupy herself in the evening. She read her favorite books, or took walks along the sea wall. Sometimes she painted or tended to the potted plants. Late in the night when it was very still, as only islands can be, she heard the surf breaking on the reef, bringing back memories of her childhood. She selected those states or feelings which gave her special pleasure and, unencumbered, she turned them in her mind as she pleased. She knew in some strange way her life at the cottage by the sea held the key to her present unease.

The cottage was a mile east of Vandrakula. On one side of it were the stately coconut groves spreading out to the hills—a series of volcanic mounds cloaked in green foliage. On the other side was the enigmatic sea. The hills entered into the sea just beyond the village. From the cottage the dark boulders looked like a herd of animals struggling out of the sea.

The cottage was built from native wood and reeds. Charles had fashioned some European-type furniture from local timber. It was always sunny in the cottage. The floor was covered with sand. She remembered Amy complaining, "There is too much sand here and too much sun." And she pulled the blinds down. Charles sat at the breakfast table, bare-chested, wearing a topee. He smiled at Elaine across the table. Charles had very brown teeth and a ginger beard. After breakfast, he disappeared in the bush with his Fijian friends.

Amy rarely went out. Everything outside the cottage seemed to clash with her feelings. Above all she avoided the beach because of sand fleas. All day she shuffled about in the cottage moaning about the heat and the smell from the village. Once every week she walked to the Chinese shop for green vegetables. She wore her hair neatly in a small bunch in the back. The rest of her person had taken on a permanently bedraggled appearance.

Charles started a small medical center at Vandrakula. Elaine knew Charles wasn't a real doctor. He had learned something about medicine in the army. She couldn't figure out why her parents had come to the islands. Once she heard her father say that every white person on the islands was either a criminal or a fugitive. She didn't believe her parents were these things.

Every Sunday Charles read to the villagers from an old Bible in a large open bure. She remembered watching the lizards slide down the massive pole in the middle of the bure and snap at the moths. After church she played with Akanisi and Mere on the beach. Amy said her hair was full of lice acquired from the two native girls.

When it rained the sea took on a mournful expression. The beach was drab and slushy. Elaine would shut herself in her bedroom and read *The Count of Monte Cristo* or *Jane Eyre*. One afternoon her parents had gone to call on the Thaggards who were trying some Angus Brahmin cows on their farm. It was raining in the sea. Elaine was reading *Jane Eyre* in her bedroom. She was so completely absorbed she could hear the ridiculing laughter of the crazy woman in the attic and the grating of a key in the door below. Just then she heard a knocking on the front door. It was like knocking in a dream. She peeked out the bedroom window. There was no one at the door. She saw Akanisi chasing after a hermit crab in the rain. Further on some villagers were riding horses on the beach.

When she heard the knocking again, she opened the front door. That was the first time she saw Senibulu. She was standing shyly behind old Radini. It was hard to say how old Seni was; later she discovered it was the most difficult thing to tell about her. She was taller than Elaine but much darker. And she wore a soiled white frock. They sat in the lounge for some time; then suddenly Radini asked if they could leave. She invited Elaine to the village. Elaine went back to her book but her mind kept wandering to Seni and Radini. She couldn't work out why they had come to see her.

Seni guided Elaine near the dark boulders from where the two volcanic shields on the side of the hills looked like giant turtles. They watched as the boulders seemed to gambol in the onrushing surf. The sun beat down most severely on the boulders: the specks of foam were soaked up as soon as they were tossed on the rocks. Seni initiated Elaine into the mysteries of the sea. Together they collected cowrie shells or followed the progress of a mollusk that had left its shell. Seni showed her sea snakes bobbing in the waves and she tried to imagine Medusa's head: Elaine learned from Seni the art of changing every situation into a legend. Sometimes Seni transformed herself into a sea goddess and raced away from her side, squealing with laughter, because she was nudged by a local demon. Elaine observed her outrageous behavior with great amazement. Charles laughed when she told him about her friend and said Seni was an elf.

She wondered why Charles said that. And why Radini asked her to regard Seni as her sister. Alone in her bedroom at night, she tried to link Seni with Marnie, her still-born sister, who was buried at sea. She had heard Amy accuse Charles of liaisons with native women. Perhaps Seni really was her sister.

Suddenly she stopped visiting the village. Charles had seen a Japanese disguised as a coolie in the hills. Amy slept with her bed pan in her room. "Time has become historic again," Charles remarked one morning at breakfast. Earlier the Thaggards had decided to sell their farm to an Indian family. Charles and Amy spent a good deal of their time with the Thaggards before they left for England. Her friendship with Seni was short-lived, but she realized that in some profound sense, which she was unable to assess even now, it had altered her whole existence.

One afternoon Elaine was alone in her room. Her parents had gone to Thaggards' farm. Elaine heard knocking on the front door. Her heart pounding, she opened the door. Radini was standing outside, alone, her head bowed. Her eyes were red with crying. Between sobs she told her about the accident at the rocks and Seni's disappearance. The villagers searched for weeks but failed to recover the body.

Elaine locked herself in her room and cried until she dozed off. When she opened her eyes it was almost dark. She heard Amy's voice in the kitchen. "You should have seen them. Near-naked in their dhoties. Sitting on the empty crates as if they were already the owners of the property. Poor Jane, she had such difficulty shooing the impertinent beggars away . . ."

She remembered the gleam in Amy's eyes as soon as the steamer touched the pier at Suva. Amy was in a beige suit, leaning on Charles' arm, observing good-humoredly the changes she already saw in streets and shops. Charles looked bored and exhausted in his clean shirt and pants. Amy kept wiping away the sweat on his red and creased neck. Elaine was sick with influenza for weeks after their arrival. She rested in bed reading and thinking about Seni and the cottage by the sea.

Amy immediately set about establishing herself in the white community, among people who she believed might be useful to them. One of her friends, Beryl, the minister's wife, found a position for Charles in the civil service. Amy's social life was somewhat spoiled by a boorish husband and daughter who was attractive enough but lacked poise, and who spoke English with a bad accent. Soon she started complaining about the smell and heat again. Charles spent most of his time drinking at clubs.

Elaine's thought returned to Ronnie and their last happy evening together. She seldom spoke to him about her Fijian friends. Ronnie seemed unenthusiastic when she mentioned them. That evening he suggested they drive to the government compound—to her "native friends." "And don't go apologize for everything, remember," he remarked cheerfully. His comments often left her feeling inadequate and maimed; that particular night she ignored his words.

The barracks were less than ten minutes drive from her apartment. The women were sitting in the yard in their florid garments when they arrived. The men had gone to fish on the reef. Their lights were visible on the sea.

Elaine was at once thrilled and surprised to see Radini there. She first saw Radini in Suva in a throng of people at the government buildings. The sky above the buildings was metallic gray. On the lawn scattered groups of people were watching, with considerable amusement, two ancient-looking Fijian women executing a tribal rite. The back of one of the women was hunched like a turtle shell. The other woman was equally short and thick. Their chanting grew more intense as Elaine drew closer. She recognized the chant dimly: it was a call to the ancestral spirits to cleanse the land. In the crowd she caught a glimpse of Radini's face, but before Elaine could call her name she disappeared behind a wall of people.

She waited for Radini to show some recognition of their past friendship. But Radini seemed cold and surly, and she deliberately ignored Ronnie. She served him a bowl of kava and immediately turned to the others and whispered something in Fijian. They tittered together, completely disregarding the visitors. Soon they started singing. Elaine clapped her hands softly as the music came back to her.

"It was like a picture-postcard," Ronnie remarked as they drove back. "The yellow moon, the soft singing, and the hush . . ."

"And friendly natives," she added, looking into his eyes.

"And friendly natives," he smiled good-naturedly, and slipped his arm around her.

The village appeared again in her dream that night. She was being dragged into the sea between the dark boulders. She woke up in fright when the flower pot fell and cracked in the bedroom, spreading red earth on the floor. Ronnie said it was the acoustics that caused the accident.

Her troubles with Ronnie started soon afterward. She was edgy the moment they arrived at the Playhouse one Saturday night. After the play Ronnie decided they ought to stay back and talk to the players. Elaine moved in the gathering, aware only of the subdued voices over the teacups that crashed against the saucers, and the clinking of heels on the polished floor. She didn't care for Ronnie's observations to the players. Nor was she interested in striving assiduously to say the right things for him. She slipped her handbag into the crook of her arm and stepped outside.

The air was clear and restful. There wasn't a sound of traffic. She stood in the garden letting the cool night penetrate her body. She remained there for a long time, totally obvious of who she was and why she was there.

Then it happened again. The leaves of the crotons began to move. A soft rustle at first, the next instant the wind leaped from the hedge to the ground in front of her, kicking and sucking and pulling at the hem of her dress. She thought she would never be able to move. Fighting against the weariness that was overtaking her, she pulled herself together and retraced her steps to the Playhouse.

She didn't speak to Ronnie in the car. She decided that moment he must leave her. She wanted to be free again. He had moved in with her on his own accord and now he had taken control over her whole existence. She wasn't going to be crushed and humiliated by him anymore. Once in the house, her distraught mind poured out all the dumb resentment it had stored up. Shocked by the violence of her reaction, he tried to calm her, holding her shoulder. "You're hypersensitive. Overwrought. Let's talk when you're calmer." She forced him away from her, without once looking at him. He sat on the edge of the bed for a long time waiting for her to take control of herself. Suddenly he dived into the bathroom, grabbing his shirt from a chair. She heard the car pull out of the yard; the next moment it sped away toward Suva. She fell on the bed and wept with humiliation and rage.

Elaine was shaken from her thoughts by a soft scurrying movement in the corridor. Someone was walking toward the kitchen, stopped when the floorboard creaked. The muscles in her stomach knotted as she held her breath and waited. The feet started to move with anxious haste toward the back door. Before the figure disappeared, she caught a glimpse of the grinning profile, the long muslin dress, and the diamonds on the fingers.

She jumped off the bed and rushed to the back door crying, "Seni . . . Senibulu!" She looked out into the yard. There was no one about except a dog dozing peacefully on the lawn. The only thing unusual was that there was too much light all around. As she turned inside, the leaves of the mango tree stirred frantically for a second and then everything was still. Next door, an Indian girl stood erect in her garden, knife in hand.

She returned to her bedroom feeling surprisingly calm. She heard a dog bark in the neighborhood. Then another and another, until the noise was like a wailing, skirmishing crowd.

The clock in the kitchen indicated 5:30 P.M. when she woke up. It was chilly and dark inside the house. She poured herself a glass of cold milk from the refrigerator and looked out the window. The clouds had turned charcoal black as night crept over the sea.

She went back to bed again. In the middle of the night she heard the waves pounding against the reef. She saw the foam splash on the dark boulders and a white line of waves receded into the cold primeval sea. Soon the pounding started again until it grew into a deafening boom. The reef cracked and the dark waters flowed into her head. She knew she was drowned.

Gamalian's Woman

Mrs. Gamalian died in her dream one fine Saturday morning.

Bamboo, who was doing the morning's errands at the market, let out a loud discordant cry that shook the vendors as they worked, and stirred the goats and fowl already drowsy under the hot sun. The wretched boy trotted home, wobbling from side to side under the groceries perched unsteadily on his head.

For weeks the neighbors avoided the old woman's shack: the children made detours around her yard to reach the common bathroom, and the women ceased to call as if the place had been struck by a plague. Night after night they watched the old woman, who had risen from the dead, and the miserable boy sitting on the veranda by a lantern. They remembered how the pundit had halted, open-mouthed, in the middle of his mantras, and the pallbearers scrambled into the guavas, as Mrs. Gamalian rose from the bamboo coffin, peered into the dark hole on the side of the hill, next to the spot where poor Gamalian was resting, and then turned to the boy.

"Stop slobbering like an orphan, child," she said, "and set me home. I'm so tired . . . and cold." She curled back into the coffin, pulling the white sheet over her. The boy gulped and wept with happiness.

Soon afterwards, the cane harvesting came to an end. The night sky was lit up with the burning fields for the last time. Trains no longer chugged and snorted at night. Dhanbhagyam, the pariah woman, was the first to call at Mrs. Gamalian's barrack. After her, Bisun's wife came, chanting to the protecting deities. Gradually, other women from the lines and the adjacent village started arriving in droves, and huddled around the old woman all day long. Bamboo loitered in the barrack beaming, immeasureably pleased with the world. The lasses from the lines crouched behind Mrs. Gamalian, unraveled her matted hair, and combed it down into long silvery strands. After her hair was combed and pasted down with coconut oil, the old woman began her narrative: always a superb maker of fiction, she brought out images that cluttered her dreams, and strung them like beads.

Mrs. Gamalian navigated her way through waves of dreams and reveries and lurched onto her gilded palanquin. Her lathi and spectacles floated in the air for a moment and then plummeted down into the yard, splashing the dew from blades of grass. The glasses were immediately covered with a film of mist.

Tears trickled down the old woman's cheeks, weeks later, as she thought of the faded magnificence of her dream palanquin. Her audience gazed at her face—a face that was bleached and lined like driftwood. Their hearts throbbed with many unarticulated fears and questions. Mrs. Gamalian stroked her feet like a weary traveler, and turned to the women who had huddled around her.

"Who could tell," she said, "if it was the sea or the air?" Although the sea wasn't her element, it never seemed to have left her alone since the day she fell into the water at the quarantine island and lost an ear. Fortunately for her, Shankaran, who had emerged from the solitary mangrove bush where she had been a moment ago, saw her struggling in the waves and rushed to her aid.

However, she heard the soughing of waves and the screeching of dark sea birds as her palanquin wandered through falling clouds and layers of empty space with strange echoes. The frozen moon glittered like a great silver plate.

Mrs. Gamalian's mind grew feverish with unwritten, disembodied tales. Her dream palanquin descended into opulent Garden-Heaven— as she had always known it—of marble sculptures spouting rainbows and sacred perfumes; giant lotuses with petals like pink silk; jewel-laden peacocks; temples, flute players, and dancers. No sooner had she staggered into the Garden, like a stranger in rags, the cosmic terror beating in her heart, when a booming voice resounded in the atmosphere, directing her toward the onion-shaped domes in the distance. She stood in the courtyard muttering, "Rama . . . Rama . . ." From one of the domes appeared the gate keeper, his eyes moving like beams of fire that lit up the old woman's face. He asked her who she was. "Kameli's woman," she answered, almost speechless. With a flash, the gate keeper disappeared through a tiny cell. Only when he had gone did

Mrs. Gamalian discover with a shudder that without his painted face and straggling curls, the gate keeper was the very image of her dead husband. She tried to superimpose the image of old Gamalian on the gate keeper, but it slid like quicksand as soon as the gate keeper returned with an enormous sheaf of paper, higher than the piles of linen in Naidu's drapery. He unrolled yard after yard of paper, running his rugged finger over rows of names, repeating hoarsely, "Kameli's woman . . . Kameli's woman . . ." Finally, he looked up at her, shook his massive curls, and said, "Your time isn't up, woman." The gate keeper lit a stove and prepared a bowl of tamarind soup and fresh saijan for her journey back to the barracks. She saw the stony mask disappear from the gate keeper's face: he was Gamalian again.

At this stage her listeners became insatiable in their curiosity; their minds hovered over the sacred paper piled up at the gate keeper's feet. Mrs. Gamalian chided the girl who tried to interrogate her too closely. She tilted her head, dropped a trickle of warm coconut oil into her dead ear, and continued musing again. The women saw a shrewd gleam in the old woman's eyes, and they retired whispering how evasive and secretive the harridan had grown.

"And deities, Kaki. Were there gods in the Garden?" asked Bisun's wife the following night. The others clucked their tongues with displeasure at the thoughtless question which distracted the old woman's mind from the gate keeper's parchment. Mrs. Gamalian felt a bewildering sensation in her head as the flute players were transformed into so many Krishnas, and the chorus girls into his maids. The gardener pulling the red hose was Indra, the god of rain. And as Mrs. Gamalian boarded her palanquin, Shiva had dismissed his dance class to repose against the blue hills.

All the deities, long-preserved in her dreams, reemerged before the old woman's eyes.

The story of Mrs. Gamalian's miraculous return reached the four corners of Vanua Levu. Many families crossed the hills, traveling through dark hours with their lanterns to reach the barracks. Some made their journey on the Colonial Sugar Refining Company's Thursday night passenger train. There were more clandestine visits by distinguished clients from the town who came with gifts. The old woman grew intoxicated with the magic of her dreams, and her passion for increasing her fortune increased accordingly. Like a crusty old usurer, she gathered her shabby gifts, and traded them for pound notes at Dukhie's store. Alone at night, she counted her lucre, laughing, feeling very wicked, till tears rolled down her cheeks.

Mrs. Gamalian's eyes roved over the yard and fastened on her dead husband's dhoties which billowed over and snapped on the clothesline.

Poor Gamalian stood before her on his bandy legs, his shiny dome as bald as a brass lota. He cupped his hands on the turf of hair on his navel, and met his clients smiling benignly, jostled by many holy thoughts. Gamalian, who had disappeared into the rain forests in search of Tantric knowledge, surviving on goat milk and green chillies for five long years, returned as a sadhu daubed in ashes and sandalwood paste, to alleviate the suffering of the slaves of this god-forsaken island. There were always ailing and diseased laborers for whom the cure—usually a pill or a laxative—doled out by the mill dispensary was of little value. There were young women whose wombs had closed unexpectedly; well-to-do men with properties who had become victims of the malevolent designs of greedy relatives; and badmash children who peed in the dark and did not spit on it, and thus had the demons follow them to their homes. They all came to Gamalian's door.

Gamalian prayed and chanted, chanted and prayed tirelessly, until his whole body swayed like a lantern battered by the wind. Slowly his eyes opened like two blazing coins, and peered into the affected organ of his client. He abused the unholy influences and spat contemptuously at the insolent demons. Mrs. Gamalian watched the bizarre performance with great fascination and obvious satisfaction. His excesses in these activities often caused her to chuckle as she plied her flour-sieve or prepared the vials for her husband's clients.

Mrs. Gamalian's thoughts returned to her palanquin, its jalousied windows and gold brocaded cushions. Dreams which originated in the arkathis' lies blossomed in her seasick mind on the swirling deck of the "Elbe." She escaped death by drowning only to be abandoned to the poorest of the labor colonies. She suffered the rogueries of the sirdars and white overseers on horseback. She survived the chronic woes brought by fearful hurricanes which tore down housetops and flooded the sugar cane. And she withstood the stings of the dreaded mosquitos that drilled fever into the blood and laid so many erect bodies to rest.

She endured all these and much more, paying in sorrow for the unalloyed happiness which, she believed, was bound to come.

Mrs. Gamalian hoed the canefields with Dhanbhagyam and Chinta, wrapped in her noon dreams. She ruminated on the arkathis' words. "You're a Brahmin woman," he said to her, "shrewd in the ways of this world and the other. You're certain to marry a merchant prince on the islands." If not a happy merchant, she could have compromised for a well-paid schoolmaster: there were many Tamil schoolmasters, clothed in pants instead of the usual dhoties and sporting softly sprouting mustaches. Why then in the name of Providence did she fall for that lout Shankaran? For a second the charred image of her first husband, black as pitch, lingered before her eyes. But she felt no pity for him.

Nor for her other husbands—Kunjrama or Muttaiya. They were all paupers. Sons of Daridra, who either deserted her or died.

She had visions of marrying according to full Brahminic rites. She despised the way Desamma and Kali carried on, sleeping with their men without proper ceremony, full of sin—how their children crawled in the fly-specked gutters! Anyway, who could blame them; there were so many men about and so few women . . .

Mrs. Gamalian's thoughts, full of dark memories, drifted to the other shadowy inhabitants of her mind. To Kunjrama, an illiterate, bent on a career in the clerical line. He filled her heart with vain hopes while he lounged around in the town, feeding on her savings and growing rounded and sleek. Every night he told her he was waiting for an important opening. On the market day, he drank from her grocery money, returning to the barracks fully inebriated and abusing her in the most vulgar tongue; she had to force him out and lock the door. One night, he veered into a ditch and never stirred again.

And what about Muttaiya, the cattle thief and gambler, who sat on his haunches in the sultry heat all day long, chewing betel nuts and carrying on his disgraceful trade after dark—what prompted Mrs. Gamalian, so full of common sense, to take him into her house? Muttaiya didn't come alone. He brought with him, lord knows how and from where, a ridiculous-looking child with knobby knees and large staring eyes. The boy would fetch firewood, do the errands, Muttaiya said, and she would live like a queen! Muttaiya disappeared as stealthily as he had come, leaving the comical creature behind. Later the knave was seen on board the "Amra," with his herd of animals, bound for Savusavu.

Yes, Gamalian was a good man, a god's man. The fact that he was devoted to her and was respected for his holiness more than atoned for his dowdiness. Together they toiled in the hot sun, living on meager rations and saving as much as possible, until their bones couldn't stand the hardship any more. They were pensioned off to a solitary barrack—a two-room shack, smelling like a warehouse. Birds nested in the ceiling. The floor creaked, the twisted roof flapped in the wind, and rain cracked into the couple's sleep.

The old woman worked with her flour sieve or wooden mortar. Gamalian plodded along to the barracks or the nearby villages to see his clients. At night she brought out Gamalian's cheelum and her almanac, and sent the boy for her glasses. She settled in front of the lantern to consult the ancient parchment. The boy lit a fire in the trunk of a dry mango tree to keep the mosquitoes at bay. He squatted on the veranda and watched the old couple until sleep cascaded upon his head. The neighbors saw Gamalian's cheelum glow in the midst of disconnected images thrown by the lantern. There were whispers of ganja and bhang. The old woman pulled at the cheelum too after their doors were shut, the neighbors said.

The old woman heard the boy cry in his dream. She removed her glasses and saw Gamalian nodding with sleep. She had seen the old man grow more absent-minded each day while her own mind became restless with wild imaginings. One night Gamalian smoked his last pipe. The old woman set his cheelum in his room by the rusty clock that didn't work.

The front door opened and shut violently in the wind. Mrs. Gamalian's thoughts returned to the broods of women who gathered at her shack every day. She had seen their numbers dwindle. Their visits too became intermittent. The women had come seeking truth and prophecy; the old woman offered only fiction. Seeing their sagging interest, her mind grew more delirious: images from her dreams fluttered like birds which she trapped into new yarns. Now she proceeded through a hiatus to the other side of her Garden—the sight of burning cauldrons and spiteful, imp-like Yamdutas with flaming rods and the agonized faces of the dead. Her audience, more alert to her contrivances now, interrupted her narration with teasing interjections.

In the years that followed, the old woman seldom moved beyond the veranda. She spent her days like a lonely eccentric with the dregs of her dreams.

Sometimes she tilted her head, as if responding to a memory, but the images were no longer alive; they seemed faded like leaves in a compost. At night she felt the dreams swirling forth from some unknown primitive spring. In the morning they dispersed like bits of paper in the wind. Gradually the storm in her dead ear died down. Her breath in her drought-ridden sleep changed into a faint trill.

One night after the neighbors had shut their doors, Mrs. Gamalian took her lantern and crawled under the veranda. She groped in a corner, sweeping away the pebbles of mud with her fingers, and started to dig. She stopped briefly when a dog barked or a siren from a train shrilled across the darkness. She continued digging until her fingers reached an earthenware jar. She pulled out the jar, unscrewed the lid, and pushed her trembling fingers through the narrow opening. Her fingers searched frantically. Alarmed at the void she felt, she hurried back into the shack and emptied the contents on a sugar bag. She lifted the lantern close to her face and looked: there were no bank notes on the sack; only fragments of old paper, some of it crumbled to dust by the action of her fingers.

The neighbors said they heard the demented cry of the crazy woman in their sleep.

Early the following morning, Mrs. Gamalian dispatched the boy to the market for tamarind and fresh saijan. She prepared a large bowl of tamarind soup and emptied the contents of the jar into the soup. A woman with a pail and a bare-backed child lingered in the yard and watched the old woman and the boy eat their soup. They heard the old woman tell the boy about the journey and how a rickety gharry would arrive to take her away. The boy asked for more soup and stared at the old woman's face, smiling incredulously.

One morning the old woman died in her shack, leaving Bamboo a bawling, bewildered orphan.

Kala

The rainy season was over. This unseasonal June rain descended on the city unexpectedly at mid-morning, by some strange godly intercession, ending the spell of drought.

Black rain erupted suddenly on the buildings, slashed into shopfronts; soon both sides of the streets were filled with running water.

And she saw him again. There at the intersection, in the first flurry of rain, thrusting through the crowd that seemed like a herd of buffalo in a mirage. He was lost temporarily. Then he re-emerged. He paused under a shop awning, frowning a little, wiping the rain off the sleeves of his yellow shirt.

The rain had made everything seem unreal. She wondered if it was the rain or her habit of seeing extraordinary significance in ordinary things that caused that feeling. Everything she saw and felt took on a dream-like quality: the excited faces that streamed in the sticky heat of the shopfronts, the generalized dread as he strode in her direction.

For a moment she was immobilized and thought she wouldn't be able to bear the encounter. Short-breathed, her temples tautly drawn, she labored under conflicting impulses: she wanted to meet his eyes, and at the same time avoid drawing attention to herself. She kept her gaze fixed on the pavement, believing, absurdly, that there was an intimacy between them that he would at once recognize, an intimacy that required no words or gestures.

Her mouth was dry, and her red blouse black with perspiration. Her face, tense and moist, gleamed with expectation. She felt a tightness building up at the back of her neck. She opened and closed her handbag nervously, rummaging through it for a handkerchief to clear her nose. She felt an unseen shadow touch her, brush over her. The pressure behind her head became intolerable. She waited desperately for the moment to jolt back to ordinariness. She saw his feet slide past her with a vague limp in their stride. She looked about furtively; he had disappeared into the crowd.

Wheels skidded in the streets. Faces behind frosted glass emerged briefly, took shape, and disappeared.

The rain had broken the city's monotony, interrupting work and stirring excitement. Someone had found a rat in the water. A crowd gathered on the pavement by the helpless creature, until a gust of wind sent rain scattering on the pavement, driving the crowd into the shops.

Holding her sari down, Kala crossed the street with a nervous haste.

After the rain a silvery haze hung over the city. Kala gazed out of the kitchen window. The sky hadn't softened. There were patches of rain on the side of the hills, and lightning flashed in the distance over the sea.

She heard water drip from the roof onto the pawpaw tree outside the kitchen window which faced the lawn. The unkempt grass was laid flat by the rain, and pools of clear water collected on mats of green. Beyond the lawn, the houses looked drenched and huddled together.

She stood at the window for a long time. Somewhere in the house a door opened with a low creak. She turned quickly, and tiptoed to the adjoining room. The child, sleeping, resembled a large bird folded within its wings.

She turned to the lounge. It was warm there, and slightly suffocating. There was still that faint unease she had sensed all week long. Sukhen's book was open under the lampshade, his slippers on the frayed rug. She shuffled back into the kitchen. Briskly she gathered the end of her sari at the waist, cleared the table of cups and left-over food, and boiled some water for the sink.

She turned on the radio and caught the final news item. They were still searching for the girl who had plunged into the Rewa River. Now the river would be swollen, making the search difficult. She pictured the girl's body washing out to sea and sinking below a ring of foam.

Poor Sukhen. She regretted she had brought up the subject of her job. Her outburst about work and self-fulfillment must have sounded so hollow. She blushed with shame as she thought of that evening. She knew she had over-played the home-bound housewife. Anyway that was after her interview with that creature from the Ministry of Education.

She felt anger building up again as she recalled the smirking face of the official. She disliked him the moment she saw him. She knew the type: insolent toward those below him but obsequious and cringing in the presence of his superiors. He was bald and impotent-looking, socks pulled up to his knees, dressed like the white colonial he had replaced.

He ignored her completely, continued to turn the flimsies in red and green folders, and answered the telephone with a secretive grin on his face. She sat awkwardly on a wooden chair under a ceiling fan that whirred feverishly. The room was newly painted, and had a half-finished appearance. When the man lifted his head, it was to announce that *his* ministry had nothing for her, and dismissed her with a nod. She left the office trembling with anger. She felt dizzy when she stepped into the sun.

Later she wished that she had had the fighting spirit, a bit of the abrasive manner, to retaliate, or at least stand up to him. She directed all her indignation at Sukhen. She was a woman who had been let down by marriage, crushed by a patriarchal system. Sukhen listened to her without saying anything. She hated him for staring at her like that, appraising her, thinking, she imagined, that it was all part of her stubbornness, her four independent years in India, and a degree in English literature. He came close to saying that once.

She had regarded her marriage as a trap. It undermined her true self. She had believed that she married for love. She was beginning to doubt even that. Things had been a little confused from the start. Sukhen had come to see her father on some business in Sigatoka. She liked Sukhen. But it was her mother who presented her with an appealing image, pointed to the aura about Sukhen—isn't he a bit like Lord Krishna himself? she said. So, when Sukhen asked Kala, she said yes she would marry him.

From the beginning, Sukhen's opinions had governed their life. In a real sense she lived his life. But she admired his mind, admired what she saw as his gift of clarity, his ability to see general meaning below ordinary occurrences. This helped her to see many things clearly herself. She willingly submitted herself to his wishes. She was told she must live for others. She had lived for her parents, Mr. and Mrs. Shiu Nath—she enjoyed referring to them thus—and for Sukhen, now for the child. This was the role decreed for the Hindu wife. In fact she found much satisfaction in it.

But she had lost much. It is true she vowed she would live for love. Now she was thinking of work and independence. Well, she had told herself, hadn't Sukhen's own life been formed by his work at the Foreign Affairs office? And hadn't he himself said you are free to be something and you are free to be nothing?

She had changed. So had Sukhen. At one time he was so full of the beauty of her inner life, her innocence and authenticity, her *Indianness*. He even said that there was something of an artist in her. She felt her world rising; it gave her the feeling there was a real self curled up somewhere inside waiting to be born. But very quickly that feeling had atrophied.

This casting about for her own voice, these counter-arguments she produced, had given her great confidence. She thought she had regained her self-esteem. She spoiled everything that night by screaming that she wouldn't have another child. Sukhen shouted back. And they quarreled as they had never quarreled before.

She thought just a few weeks ago she was completely satisfied with this unexamined life; now through her own doings she had brought chaos into their life. She could never think unkindly of Sukhen. It wasn't Sukhen, it was the emptiness of her life that unsettled her. Still she had his love; that was one real thing in her life. There was also something else: her education had given her the ability to use other people's views; living with Sukhen had agitated her to find out things for herself. Somehow he made her feel whole. Sometimes she wished he didn't have such an influence over her.

When Sukhen returned from work she clung to him, overpowered by her tears. She didn't want a life in which their love wasn't the center.

She prepared dinner while he read the paper. She watched him slumped on the sofa in his baggy work pants, his head propped on his arm. She had watched him like that often, always feeling great tenderness. I love him, she said, and I will die a thousand times for him. She crossed the lounge wiping her wet hand on her sari. She stood by the couch looking into his moist brown eyes. She tilted her head smiling, saw how awkwardly his mustache was perched on his face; she hadn't quite adjusted to the new image it produced. She kneeled on the floor, still smiling, thinking of the clumsy adolescent verse he had written for her:

> *If you hadn't come in my life*
> *I'd have died*
> *Without anyone kissing my eyes.*

She smoothed his forehead, ran her fingers through his tousled hair, and kissed his eyes.

She returned to the kitchen, happy with this sudden outpouring of softness, this special closeness.

The sky was still hard. She saw there was barely any light there. Gradually the neighborhood darkened. Somewhere children were playing in the dusk. A baby squealed from a house, and then a sharp female voice rang out.

Slowly luminosity returned, now from the lighted windows. Beyond the houses wings of darkness spread to the bleakly lit streets. She heard a car grunt, saw it move slowly on the shiny asphalt, and disappear around the bend. In the twilight of the lampposts, the silhouetted figure of a man hurried in the same direction.

Her gaze returned to the lounge. Sukhen wasn't on the couch. For a second she felt frantic, as if she had lost him for good. She called his name and rushed into the bedroom, pushed open the bathroom door, swerved into the adjacent room. He was kneeling by the child's cot, watching her soft, regular breathing. He looked up without saying anything. She pulled him roughly to her and clung to him.

The following morning she took the child to Sukhen's mother, and caught a taxi to the city.

A cold wind swept the half-empty streets. The city had a bright, scrubbed look; it glowed coldly in the midmorning sun. She strolled uptown, along shopfronts, gazing into shop windows, sickened by the sight of stale cake in a glass cage.

She entered a side street of old shops. A soft gloom hung over this part of the city. She picked her way along the broken pavement and dug-up mud, fearing knowing looks or lewd remarks from the two road laborers who leaned on their shovels and chatted with a tall Fijian in blue overalls and large mauled boots. She walked under a scaffolding, avoiding the rubble from a collapsed facade. The dreary shopfronts were about to receive a face lift. The Fijian grinned as she walked past him.

She cursed herself for taking this street. Further on, a couple of men were knocking down a concrete wall. Their hands were covered with plaster. She stopped briefly to watch a black cat climb a flight of broken steps to reach a sunny spot. She hurried across the street when a shopkeeper, with dark bloated face, lips lined with betelnut juice, stared disapprovingly at her.

The shopkeeper turned to talk to the Fijian in blue overalls, who was now sitting at the bottom of a dark stairway that led to well-lit offices displayed behind French windows. She was conscious they were following her with their eyes. She looked back. The shopkeeper had gone inside. The Fijian was still grinning. She bit her lips and smiled back. The Fijian laughed explosively, shaking his grizzled head. A flash of white showed between her lips as she laughed unabashedly, a rich and easy laughter. The workmen stopped pounding the wall and started to gaze in her direction.

She smiled to herself at this absurd exchange, and strolled on through clusters of people at the busy supermarket. She paused on the bridge across Nabukalou Creek. The sour-looking stream, lined with black and green bricks and rusted iron, moved sluggishly with the refuse. It bore the stench of rotting mangroves.

She stood there for some time, her head in a daze. The lonely haunted face she had seen emerge from the black rain swam before her eyes. She saw a pair of bare feet on naked shingles slaked with rain. Again she experienced the strange spell of those feet that had ages of solitude moving with them. She wanted to touch them, wash them of their weariness and sorrow with her tears. When she became conscious of her surroundings, her face burned with shame. She wandered through the streets, sobbing inwardly, afraid of the madness that was overwhelming her.

Her legs ached. She felt shabby; her hair was askew, and her face gleamed with perspiration. She looked for a place to rest, found an empty table at the less crowded end of a milk bar. She leaned back on her chair wearily, with half-closed eyes, wondering why she was there. She seemed to be pushed along as in a dream; she could not retreat, and what lay ahead seemed dim and frightening.

An elderly waitress wiped the table with a dirty sponge, without looking at her or showing any interest in taking an order. She dropped her elbows on the table, pressing her temples with her fingers, digging into her thick black hair.

Opposite her table two men sipped tea from large white cups. The man in florid shirt and shorts suffered from a bad cold. His companion, bearded, wearing dark glasses, was reading from a wad of pink papers. He had a tense expression. The other poured tea from a battered tin teapot. He had a witty mouth and nodded frequently. After pouring the tea, he pulled a newspaper from his pocket and, just as deliberately as he had poured the tea, he spread the newspaper on the table. He pulled the sheath of pink papers to his side, marked a section with a blue pen, and drew his friend's attention to the photograph on the front page of the newspaper.

Kala watched the two men for a while, then abruptly crossed over to the counter for a newspaper and returned to her table. The photograph on the front page was of an accident: a man sprawled on the wet asphalt before a semi-circle of agitated spectators, seen through a skein of rain which glistened in the headlight of a car.

She stared at the photograph for a long time, then turned the page. The drowned girl had surfaced. She had left a note: she had gone to join her dark lover in Brindaban.

Kala read the story again on the bus. Her mind kept returning to the girl's story. It triggered her memory, sent it racing into the past, into the bittersweet agony of her childhood infatuation with the dark god. She saw the bent figure of her Vashnavite grandfather, recalled his mocking smile, his virahdukha songs about the god and his herd-girls. One morning, when she had come to his side, freshly bathed for prayer, her hair damp and loose on her shoulder, he made her sit on his string bed and sing to him. She sang in her plaintive voice her favorite song "My Mate Is He." Without her knowing, the old man had invested her fantasies with real emotions and feelings. And dressed in that role for the school concert, of a rural lass forsaken by her god, she actually felt affected by his fickleness. Her teachers said she had real talent. She was so happy. She held the old man and sang to him. She recalled laughing and running away when he tried to hold her by his side.

She alighted at the bus stop in her street, and returned to the house intoning lines from the old song.

The meandering in the city left her feeling tired and unclean. She washed, put on an attractive sari, and waited for Sukhen.

She gazed at the neat, whitewashed house next door. She saw Sumintra and Gopal enter with bags of groceries. They had finished work early. There was movement in the kitchen, and, after a while, the house was surrounded by a suffocating gloom. She wished she could talk to Sumintra, woman to woman. But after her first overture of friendship, which finished in a near-catastrophe, she decided to keep away from her. She had seen Sumintra on weekends, sitting at the door, legs spread out, as if seized by an incurable boredom, and Gopal moving about looking sallow and defeated. Yet they had married for love.

It is like this with life, Kala told herself. It either ends in sterility and boredom or leads to daily torment. Looking at the still house now, she wished it would explode and free the couple from where they were so cruelly imprisoned.

Kala too had loved destructively. She saw it clearly. She had told herself she was saving Sukhen from his clamoring, clutching relatives; whereas, in fact, she wanted him all for herself. But she had managed to overcome her fears, realizing that these fears could only stifle love, which had a chance only in freedom. Sukhen loved differently. He had suffered much as a child, and again during his studies abroad, and had come close to what he called "the enticement of the great emptiness." Sometimes she witnessed a disquieting aloofness which frightened her. Love assuaged his pain, diminished his anxieties. She loved him more because he needed her.

Sometimes she had wished for a special intensity, and was disappointed with his sober love. But his face had so many subtle expressions, so many moods. She wanted him to be simple, someone who would love and be loved. When she broke free of her self-centered, narcissistic love she started to appreciate the beauty of his friendship. She found him pure-hearted, someone who would love without wanting any reward. She did have many moments of intense happiness with him. During those early days they listened to music a lot, and talked most of the night. She loved listening to him. His words had the magical quality of lifting all their experiences above the mundane, of refining what was crudely lived. He called himself a colonial betrayed by history. She loved even his despair. Then there were those beautiful details about his childhood which made her laugh and cry at once. When they had their first car, they drove around the island and picnicked along the coast. Sukhen showed great patience during these outings and attended to every detail.

After her wanderings in the city, she felt her actions had betrayed their extraordinary intimacy. She wanted to tell him everything, talk to him about what was happening to her. She decided to wait until he returned from his trip abroad.

The two weeks Sukhen was away she returned to the city. She moved alone in the crowd, absent-mindedly, among malingerers, hangers-on, tourists—all performing their rites. So many empty faces, so many people footloose in the streets. She returned home when the sidewalks started to empty, her face burning with shame. Standing by the kitchen window, while the child played in the lounge, she felt the sadness of early nightfall. She was never so lonely or lost.

She fed the child, eating very little herself. She locked herself with the child in the bedroom, and gave herself up to morbid thoughts about madness and death. One night she woke up, sweating, to the phantasmal stillness of the house. Her forehead was in a fever. She lit a table lamp. She leaned against the wall, slowly slid down onto the floor, and sat there clenching her fists, feeling that if she didn't do something she would be engulfed by emptiness. She would never be herself again. She made up her mind to call Bijma, her younger sister, who lived in Sigatoka. Bijma sometimes stayed with her when Sukhen went abroad.

The following morning was bright and warm. She stood before the red mirror, ran her fingers over the curve of her cheek, studied her eyes. Both her face and eyes had retained a girlish radiance in spite of her thirty-two years. She felt a youthful glow invade her body. She forgot about Bijma, and started to enjoy the freedom of her aloneness.

She had lived in Suva for over seven years, yet she hadn't seen the city fully. In fact she had avoided it, regarded it as featureless, existing only for money. It was unlike the cities she had holidayed in during university vacations in India. These cities were full of myth and history. Now as she broke free of her sheltered life, the city suddenly took on a romantic aspect; it seemed to contain an extraordinary amalgam of feelings and sensations. It started to open up, come under her control.

She did things she hadn't done before. On impulse she opened her first bank account. And overcome by an impetuous feeling, she dropped a coin into the metallic box of an acrid-smelling public telephone, dialed a number at random, and carried on a conversation with a perfect stranger.

She strolled by the market stalls and push-carts, laughing at the ritual mutterings of the peanut sellers at the grimy bus station. She stood in the strong wind at the harbor, and watched a ship decked with tourists wearing seashell jewelry. She didn't feel befouled passing through the ill-famed alleys of the city.

One afternoon she walked into the city library, told herself she'd read something really outrageous. She searched through the shelves, reading odd pages from books she picked up. She selected a volume, carried it to an empty table, and read through an entire segment entitled "Diary of the Seducer."

It seemed to her that, in the city, she had strayed into a hidden region, the dark underside of her existence, where she was taken beyond daily responses into another mode of feeling. But she was never far away from the elusive shadow. For some obscure reason she imagined him sick and dying, and needing her help. What if he had tried to contact her and she hadn't known? She expected a glimpse of him in the long mirrors in Cumming Street, in an empty parking lot in a brown overcoat, or sitting on the sea wall against a flight of gulls and a dying afternoon.

She found him in her dream on a red hilltop, crawling upward on the bare slope like a fugitive, and she slipping and falling, her face smeared with red earth.

She asked herself what if he should overtake her one day, halt in front of her, touch her hand? She would melt on the pavement. Perhaps he would shake her by the shoulder and wake her from her dream.

Then she saw him. He was in a bookstore at the counter, his back toward her at an angle. She stood by a shelf of books in a state of near-panic, without moving or even turning her face. For a breathless second, out of the corner of her eye, she saw his outstretched hand on the counter. A hand she had touched so many times in her mind, the arch of his wrist, bones of his fingers, tendons, veins, the soft flesh brazened by the weather. A strong masculine hand. It waited furtively to receive the change. She shuddered when he spoke to the attendant. She couldn't catch the words, but the voice was cracked and troubled, and seemed to emanate from some remote corner of his being.

Suddenly he turned toward the door. A quick surreptitious movement of her eyes, and she caught a glimpse of one side of his bearded face and head. His hair had a touch of gray. The next instant he hurried away as if fleeing from something.

She took a deep breath and stepped outside the bookstore. It was bright in the street. She ran to the sidewalk. She saw him moving quickly in the crowd, shielding his eyes with a newspaper. His rapid stride accentuated the limp in his right foot. Soon he was lost in the pavement crowd. She stood motionless on the sidewalk, feeling a flush of breeze sweep over her.

She waited for Sukhen at the airport. She felt nervous and unsteady, and thought what if he wasn't on the plane. Suddenly he was there at the exit by the flight attendant. He chatted energetically all the way to Suva, with a happy glint in his eyes. She was mostly silent, her mind drifting off, sometimes looking at his face, sometimes gazing out of the car window.

They had an early dinner. She took the child to her room, and washed and dried the dishes. Sukhen showered, and settled into bed with the fortnight's newspapers.

She sat on the edge of the bed stroking his feet. Gently she prepared him, careful at first not to say too much or too little. She told him everything, and how lonely and confused she had been.

He placed the newspaper slowly onto his lap, and stared into her face. "I don't understand what it is all about, Sukhen, I really don't . . . . Couldn't it be that it's all a daydream?"

"Tell me what you think," he said, narrowing his eyes but without appearing to force her to respond. He folded the newspapers and dropped them onto the floor. She saw he had paled. She tried to avoid his gaze, afraid of those far-seeing eyes.

"Sukhen, you'll have to help me . . ." Her throat was full. She was ready to burst into tears.

"But you had gone to the city several times, that much seems clear," he said. She sensed the deep irritation in his voice. He was starting to look at her from an immense distance. Lord, how could he be so cold and objective. She had great difficulty controlling her speech. He continued to peer at her. She was relieved when he withdrew his eyes. A prolonged silence followed when the specter she had created seemed to govern their thoughts.

She reached for his shoulder. His body flinched slightly. After a moment he disengaged himself without looking at her. She tried to hold his hand but he lurched past her. She saw him walk to the creek behind the house, and stand at the edge of the creeping wilderness.

She found her slippers, and went out to the porch. The night was dark, full of stars, and the grass moist with dew. She sat on the step, her face cupped in her hands. After several minutes she lifted her face. She clasped her elbows as a shot of chill pierced her body. He was still gazing into the black emptiness.

He walked slowly back, and crouched in front of her. He took her limp fingers into his hand without looking at her. She saw he was reaching out. She wanted to hold him and cry freely. He raised his eyes, watched the play of light in her eyes, in her nightblue hair. His lips broke into a half-smile. Unable to contain her tears, she wept openly, burying her hot face in his shoulder. He led her into the house.

She heard him sleeping deeply. She lay on her back, hands beneath her head, legs pulled up under the sheet. She was seized by a sudden desire to grow old, allow her flesh to frizzle and fade away. This would be preferable to witnessing the rapid corrosion of her love. Her face was wet with tears.

She got up early in the morning, washed, and combed her hair, not forgetting to apply red dust on the white parting in her hair. She prepared his breakfast. Sukhen took an inordinately long time in the shower, fidgeted in the drawers, which irritated her because she wanted him to eat his breakfast hot.

Throughout the week he was edgy. She had difficulty assessing his true feelings. When he spoke he was vague and uncertain. There was an air of irreconcilable strife in the house. At night, she listened to some music while he read, seated in his customary chair. They slept on the two sides of the bed, apart.

Saturday morning they remained in bed together. The child appeared at the half-open door rubbing her eyes, hesitated, then waddled to her room. When Kala looked in, the child was asleep again. After a few minutes she returned to bed. There was warmth and pleasure in the crumpled sheet. She pulled it over their bodies, propped her head on the pillow, and turned sideways toward him. He had that half-smile on his face. He rolled on his side, stroked her face, running his fingers over her nose, the lovely arch of her cheekbone, felt her warm hair, her warmly stirring body. He fixed his gaze on her kohled eyes. Her face was flushed and yielding, and he kissed her, drawing her to him. She recalled now that he had said to her once that we can love like humans and like gods. She felt they had come together after an interval of many months.

Suddenly her face burst to life. She pulled his face roughly toward hers. "Tell me," she said, "what is that one thing for which you would give your life?"

He was silent for a second, surprised at the intensity in her voice. He grinned and leaned over her, one arm across her breast. Looking into her smiling face he said, "You really want me to answer that?"

She nodded, pressing her lips.

"Perhaps for love," he said. "Because it wouldn't be for a place or any cause."

"Do you still love me, Sukhen? I mean truly love me?" she asked abruptly.

"Do you *feel* that I love you?" he replied.

"Yes, I think you must love me . . . love me very much. I don't know why . . ." Then she said, "Do you love me enough to die for me?" She appeared embarrassed at having asked that question.

"No," he responded, quickly, touching her nose, "because I'd want to live for you."

She made a coy gesture, wrinkled her nose, and inched away slightly. She gazed through the half-open window.

"What is it, Sukhen," she asked when she turned to him. "What is it that we want? Why am I so uncertain?" She broke off, covered her face with her hands, pulling at the sheet.

He held her hand on the pillow and said, "Isn't it something like this: all we can know is that we are here now, and then there is nothing. And what we have between now and that nothing is our love. That is the only thing."

Tears clouded the pink of her eyes. "Isn't it our duty, then, to be happy?" She held him, crying inwardly. "What will become of us, Sukhen . . ."

When she took hold of herself, she found both her heart and mind responding to his words as if she, too, through a different route, had arrived at the same meaning, and for the moment love, nameless, unutterable, whatever its total significance, seemed the natural anchorage, the only refuge from other illusions.

She waited for Sukhen on Monday. The child was by her side on the couch, in a clean dotted frock, rocking to and fro. She made Sukhen's tea, and when he was settled on the couch, she told him. There was an accident in the city. Early in the morning when it was still dark. They had found him face down on the wet asphalt, a few yards from the creek, down a skew. There was a slight wind; his brown overcoat flapped and billowed. That's how they spotted him. There was no sign of any wound on his body, only a trace of blood on his shoe. A small crowd gathered around him. Then it started to drizzle again. They took shelter under the shopfronts from where they saw his body put into an ambulance.

Sukhen kept his eyes on her face. Her nostrils flared with her breath. She did not say anything more. There was no need to explain.

What the derelict god meant to her required no naming. Like love. And Sukhen didn't say a word.

Gone Bush

a novella

Artists of the Sea

—In the beginning was the sea.
Your eyes scanned the rock-tip of a small windswept island.
—Everything came out of the sea, and that, Anandi, my friend, is the pole gods used to churn storms of fire and water. From it came the goddess of life.

We were at the curve on the beach where the shore was open. On one side was a Fijian village fringed with water-logged mangroves, and all about us was sand and beach shrubs. The sea gleamed like an immense lake under a cloudless afternoon sky.

I was starting to recognize the games your mind played. I developed the narrative, my thoughts turning to our ends and beginnings.

—From the sea also came the physicians of the gods.

I saw you staring at the waves again. How intensely you could feel the sea! Yet you seemed to me someone from a landlocked culture whose people were riders of horses. You were the romantic hero of a dimly-remembered Hindi novel. An atavistic reminder in a broken world. Always close to me, like a friend from childhood.

You came to my room with your doctor's bag that desultory July-August season of drought and fever. My mind was in a flame. I suffered another round of that creeping sense of annihilation. I was in a bad way. You held my arm and took my temperature. My eyes were fixed on the golden letters on your bag: Dr. Basant Mithra. You came with your bag every evening straight from the hospital. I waited for your car, followed your footsteps up the bare stairs. I hungered for your friendship. Twice you came with your wife Moina. She was beautiful as I had thought. She had large lustrous eyes and an attractive inward smile. She tidied up the room while you made coffee, and we sat around a small table in the kitchen and talked. One evening you found me feverish and sweating on the green carpet. You helped me to the bed. I heard you phoning Moina. When I woke up past midnight, I found you lying by the phonograph in your green shirt and cream trousers listening to sarodh music. I returned to bed feeling grateful that you were in the house.

I felt I was on speaking terms with myself again.

I recovered quickly. You said to me,

—Anandi, I'll show you a place that'll truly lift your heart.

You drove me to a secluded beach five miles out of the city. Such a hidden spot of beauty it was! You came here for your Sunday run, and for picnics with Moina. We walked on the beach till the night came.

We went there again on a Friday afternoon. We had started to walk briskly at the water's edge when a dense cloud descended over the sea and rain came down heavily. We crossed a wooden fence and hurried into a boat shed. There was a primitive dugout inside the shed with "Seafarer" carved roughly on its side. The boat was sprinkled with petals of red flowers. I held your elbow. You laughed looking at me.

—It's a Friday sea ritual.

You examined the dugout.

—Do you know I'm learning the rudiments of sailing with Sai? Sai is a pathologist at the hospital. A true artist of the sea. Some weekends we drive to his farm in Nadroga.

—Isn't sailing dangerous?

—Actually it's quite simple. A lot depends on force and reaction. But you have to trust the planks and the wind. And you should be able to read the skies at night. As Sai says, there are laws.

And why, I thought, was the sea such a part of our fears?

You were quiet for a moment.

—But in the end no one really knows how a boat sails, you said.

We sat on the dugout and watched the sea through a screen of rain. I said,

—What were the lines you were saying on the beach—they seemed so exquisite.

—Byron. They're from Sai's favorite poet.

The sea was a velvet black. When the clouds lifted, the tide came in. The sun appeared briefly, big and flaming, and then slowly melted at the ocean's rim. The sea changed from velvet to orange and red. A cluster of rocks was suddenly illuminated, a bright and warm place to absorb all the seamoods.

The sea was full of illusions that Friday. The images rose and died quickly in the water.

For a week that December we holidayed around the island in a rented car. Moina had gone to visit her parents in Australia. We took the dirt road avoiding the work-bound traffic on the sealed highway. There were abrupt bends, and sometimes the branch roads led to beach tracks, so attractive to us, or they ended up at a village or someone's yard. We turned and drove on without wanting to arrive anywhere. The gravel was damp with dew; still the car stirred puffs of dust. The trees and houses along the road waited for rain to wash off the dust.

At midday we stopped in a hot sleepy town. It was a small market town but there were not many shoppers about. We strode into an eating shop which was like a tiny arcade. Business did not seem good, yet the owner was not at all interested in us. He was perched on a high stool, wiping the sweat from the folds of his neck with a dishrag. He shouted our order to his wife in the kitchen. A ceiling fan puffed warm air on our faces.

Clutching the greasy parcels, we made our way to the sea. We quickly found an attractive tract of beach. It was a bright day for the seaside but there weren't any picnickers. We sat under the shade of a wind-scoured bush. The beach was a vast expanse of sand collected in fine heaps like low dunes. Sometimes gusts of wind blew the sand like seaspray.

Later we walked on a bed of crumpled cowries. The surf broke only yards away. You described a night sea-journey with Sai. While you talked, those lines returned to me again. Your eyes shining, you repeated them for me:

Man marks the earth with ruin—his control
Stops with the shore.

We stopped where the wind whipped a tangle of rusted wires on bleached and reclining posts.

We drove past a row of beach bungalows hidden behind dusty

hedges, and through derelict villages. We spent the afternoon in the hills between rain forests. The smell of bush came through the damp undergrowth of ferns and orchids. The road was more difficult now, and the engine sounded overstrained, and halted. We stopped to allow it to cool.

Over the high trees a flock of brightly-winged birds made a wild skirmish into the open sky.

From the top of the hill the sea showed a line of froth. We rolled down a narrow winding road into a scrubland. A dozen small wooden shacks lined the two sides of the road. Farther on, the road wound through scantily clad low hills. Toward the coast it ran between patches of mangroves and coconut palms, and through villages that were becoming shanty towns.

At dusk we checked in at a coastal hotel. It had a high-ceilinged lobby and stacks of rooms painted in tropical colors. There was a whirl of activity about the thatched bar and the palmshrouded pool overlooking the sea, in preparation for the evening. We drank beer at the thatched bar and then plunged into the pool.

When we came up the hotel was lit like an unfamiliar town. We walked through a blue-carpeted alley, the smell of the pool clinging to our bodies.

We ate a large hotel dinner and then lingered in the bar. We picked a spot overlooking the bandstand, chewed nuts, and drank beer. There was still a lot of coming and going in the lobby and luggage was being wheeled about.

The band started to play. The atmosphere was filled with the expectation of something unusual and exciting about to happen. You were in that high-spirited, inventive mood again. Your attention was fixed on a woman who was ordering a drink at the bar. She had a pink cashmere cardigan over her shoulders.

—Australian schoolteacher, you said. Her first trip abroad and she's determined not to miss a thing.

—And her husband? I asked.

—He's a missionary, you smiled gravely.

She negotiated between tables and made her way toward us. You found her a chair. She bowed and smiled and introduced herself. She was Grace Hart from Tasmania. She and her husband Sidney were teaching in Suva. This was their first holiday in three years.

—Sidney is in the room, she told us goodnaturedly. He's all peeled. He was in the sun all day.

She lay back in the chair, enquired about our work, and places to visit along the coast. Soon her attention was drawn to the dancers—so picturesque in their island costumes. She was lost in the exotic drama and music of the dances. Suddenly she remembered the following morning's cruise to the atolls. She got up abruptly. Before she hurried away she showed off her Polaroid and made us pose for pictures.

We sauntered out onto the terrace. The air was humid and we started to perspire. We looked down on the beach where some revelers were burning dried coconut fronds. They seemed like gnats swarming around a fire. We clambered down with several bottles of beer and joined the merrymakers. They were tourists and young Fijians from the nearby village. The tourist girls picked up the flaming fronds and romped about till the leaves were burned out.

After they had gone, we sat on the sandgrass tossing driftwood into the fire.

I described my half-lived life. You told me about your father.

—I think more about him lately. Something bothered him before he died. He couldn't read or write so he didn't put it down. Nor was he the sort to tell anyone. When he started to neglect the farm, we said he was tired after working it for so many years. But this sudden interest in the sea was strange to us. Sometimes he returned with fish bought on the roadside. He wasn't a fisherman.

I recalled the tense and frightened face of the old man in a photograph in your office.

—What do you think really happened?

—The reef was never safe. The Fijian villagers say many superstitious things. Perhaps he was just swept away by the tide.

I listened to your voice above the sucking and rushing of the receding tide, and thought how similar are these turning points that unmake or restore our lives: a chance scholarship saved you, as it saved me, from the fate of being just absorbed in other families.

The water was gently illuminated at the sea's edge and waves flashed like fish. The wind rose and we climbed back. The hotel waited for us like a giant ship at harbor. We tiptoed into the after-hour bar where couples were talking in soft whispers. We asked for beer, and drank till well after midnight and staggered into our room, thoroughly soused and hugging each other in our drunkenness.

You threw yourself full-length onto the bed. I sat on the edge for a while. You were falling into sleep but suddenly you turned on your side and held my arm.

—Tell me about Gaytri.

I laughed.

—Gaytri was a wrathful bitch.

You rolled on your back.

—No. Gaytri was a Circe.

—She didn't change me into a monster.

—When love ends, you have to accept it joyfully in the same heart as its beginning. Who said that?

You paused and grinned obscurely.

—Moina is a chameleon. A beautiful bright chameleon.

You babbled on. You got up and pulled your clothes off and slipped under the sheet. Since my sickness I slept with my clothes on for fear that I might have to take flight suddenly.

In my broken half-sleep, I heard the night wind, and a couple's laughter in the corridor. I opened my eyes and wondered where I was. You were sleeping deeply, your right hand resting on my shoulder.

You got up before dawn. I went out to the terrace to clear my head. The tide was out. The morning broke over the hills and shimmered on the water's surface. You were strolling to the farther end of the beach, your pants rolled up. You watched a heron kreen and make an arc, then hurried to talk to two fishermen who were rowing out in an open boat. You were in the water. The boat drifted slowly toward the reef. Now you were close to the breakers. I saw the waves riding high toward you. I ran out to the beach. I shouted again. You saw me and started to stumble away from the pursuing waves.

You stood before me, visibly impatient, and said,

—I thought something had happened.

You frowned and headed toward the hotel, leaving me feeling helpless, like a drowning man.

We gathered our things and stepped out into the blinding light. The hotel, a miniature city at night, seemed like an empty mall. We passed the landscaped golf course which languished in the first wave of heat. Along the road the morning gleamed crisply on the trees.

We drove straight into a rainstorm. Rain slapped on the glass and fell darkly on the road. You drove with concentration, your face close to the frosted windscreen. The tires started to slush mud. I broke a bottle of beer, which left a stale smell on the carpet.

You pulled off on a branch road beside a small grocery store. You rushed out onto the rainswept veranda. You bantered with the shopkeeper. After a while you returned with more chilled beer. We drank from the bottle, and waited for the rain to abate.

Before midday we headed west out of the rain. The sun broke through, high up in the sky. We rounded the coast, waving at the villagers who responded with friendly grimaces, and sped into the open country of green sugar cane fields banked by smooth treeless hills. I remarked on the inviting beauty of the landscape. You smiled, looking into my face. I

was beginning to respond to a reality you had created for me. You explained how to make good time.
—But we aren't going anywhere, I exclaimed.
You drove on, enjoying the straight and open road. Through the haze of heat we saw a group of men in farm clothes at the roadside. As we drew nearer to them, you said,
—We'll stop. A couple of them are Sai's men.
You got out of the car and shook their hands and gave them beer. You enquired about farming. They held the bottles with root-like fingers and smiled skeptically.
A lad in white clothes was going out to the sea.
—But you have no gear, I said.
He laughed, revealing a set of white teeth against dark features. He pointed to a woman struggling with a huge net at the edge of the sugar cane field.
When we got into the car again you were filled with unbounded love.
—We shall hail farmers and fishermen, you cried as we drove away.
We stopped in the next town; we wandered aimlessly in the market. We ate sandwiches and drank beer at an old hotel. The sun glared on our faces when we started again. At the sandhills we raced with a herd of wild horses. The engine halted again. The horses galloped away. We sought help at a small garage by a timberyard. The farmers we had met by the roadside cheered from a tar-smeared lorry as it sped past us.
The afternoon thickened in the pine forest. I saw clothes hanging from lines by empty houses, casting afternoon sadness in the yards. The light in the sky over the town faded and night fell suddenly on the road. We followed embers of light from the traffic moving into the town.
We washed at a motel and returned to the town for dinner. I ordered the food while you went to look for a phone to call Moina. I gazed at the sedate furniture, sipping iced water, and thinking of that other evening when we had celebrated your birthday. Every object in the restaurant had a reddish hue. There were many happy families eating. They broke frequently into joyful laughter. You wore a white jacket over a blue shirt and cream pants. Moina was in a pink sari. She had a gold chain around her neck. Both the sari and the gold chain matched splendidly her rich brown skin. You poured the wine, and played your boyish antics, switching glasses and making witty remarks to distract us. Moina laughed openly a couple of times, then checked herself, holding your arm. She looked at you with so much love in her eyes. You sauntered to the bar, and returned with two scented cigars. You offered me one. I refused. We protested wildly but you lit one, and blew a stream of smoke over the table. The families next to our table joined in the fun. Waving the smoke with your hand, you reached across the table to push away a

strand of hair from Moina's face. She blushed, and drawing your hand on the table said,

—Dr. Mithra, you've got me drunk.

—Then we will dance, you smiled, holding my shoulder.

Moina hung on your arm as we walked back to the car. You slipped your arm around her. We drove to a seaside hotel and danced till our feet felt limp with weariness. On the way back you hummed a romantic tune and urged us to sing. We sang noisily together.

You returned after phoning Moina. Your clear unmarked face seemed a tinge darker, and your eyes showed fatigue. We finished dinner quickly, and returned to the motel.

I stayed in the motel for a few days. You had assignments at the hospitals and relatives to see. I walked to the town in the morning, wandered in the bookshops, and returned with a pile of books. I read and slept.

At the end of the week we were on the northern end of the island. The sky remained open, but the climate became desolate.

The road was freshly spread with gravel, forcing us to move slowly.

We entered the talasiga country. Clumps of gasau appeared on the slopes of stony hills. The broken plateaus were filled with sun and heat. You told me about Degei, the deity who broke off a piece of the hills at Uluda to get a clear view of the sea. We gazed at a high ridge from where disembodied souls leaped into another existence.

There were bush fires farther ahead. We passed a searing hill. From the southern slopes bundles of smoke rose upward. They disappeared quickly: the sky above remained clear and blue.

We swung onto the road to a featureless half-made town squatting in the heat like some abandoned heap. Past the town, the car swerved onto a rutted lane after crossing an unused railway line. The rough farmland on both sides of the lane had a shaggy appearance. By one farm, a solitary cow gazed at us in a trance.

We stopped in the middle of a stretch of uncultivated farmland. You got out, and walked to the abandoned farmhouse. After surveying the surroundings, you disappeared inside and took a long time coming out. You waded in the tall grass, and found a farm machine partly buried in animal droppings. I crossed the yard overgrown with coarse weeds.

—There was a water tank here, you said excitedly.

You searched frantically, flattening the grass with your feet.

—Someone has carried away the water tank, you cried.

Suddenly, as if seized by some powerful memory, you moved

toward a bush of flowering nettles behind the house. I followed you, and found myself standing beside you on the soft grassy bank of a stream of great beauty. The water rolled gently over black stones in front of us, and farther down, where the stream deepened, it glinted in the broken light between the watchful, aging ivi trees laden with green fruit. Their snake-like roots slithered into the water. There was tense silence by the trees: a spider dropping onto the water would have startled us.

After a long pause you said:

—Isn't it strange, I came here as a boy because of the stream's attraction. Yet I was always very afraid. I have often asked why is it so surrounded by attractive, beautiful things. I don't know what fears my father had, though, he kept us away from the stream. The water here excites bile, he told us. He built a small water tank for us by the house.

When we climbed back, I wanted to look into the house. There were more surprises inside. It seemed to me that, like a trickster playing with illusions, you had arranged these signs to baffle the imagination. The inside of the house was not at all as I had expected. The crisscross of rafters and purlins, of strong unsawn timber lashed together with bush vines, was still impressive. The carefully braced grid was almost perfect. Only the grass on it was sodden. The mud floor, although cracked in places, was firm and unimpaired.

The door creaked. You held my arm to keep me still. I followed your eyes to a frayed sugar bag that hung from the woven inner thatch. We waited. The sack moved again, revealing a small pair of powerful talons. We shifted quietly toward the wall. Now we saw clearly the magnificent talons, thighs, plumage, and the agile head. The bird was perched on a beam like a totem.

First the stream, now this endangered falcon in this deserted surrounding—the hidden magic of the place was slowly revealing itself, it seemed, evoking the same intense pleasure and fear. After a while, as I was about to withdraw, my eyes caught the castings of bones and fur of a flying fox. I realized it wasn't the bush fire that had driven the falcon from its aerie.

From the car I saw you coming out of the ruin like a lonely survivor. Starting the engine, you smiled and said,

—Do you know the peregrine falcon is worth $45,000? At Ram Dhan's Falconry in West Germany, you might earn even more. A gyr falcon would certainly fetch you twice that amount. It's all illegal of course, but Ram Dhan takes care of everything. He migrated from this very part of Viti Levu twenty-five years ago.

You picked a hill with a clear view of the sea for us to have lunch. An old man was climbing the hill above the road. He had a cutlass in one hand. He looked down when he reached the brow of the hill. You got out of the car and strolled across to the edge of the road, waving at the old man. He saw you and started to climb down. He was excited to find you there.

While you talked to the old man, my eyes followed a coastal path below that led to the muddy foreshore. The water was low, and the reef protruded. Beyond the reef, on the eastern side, was a chain of islands, green and fringed with golden sand, floating in the blue water. A seabird rasped in the magroves.

The old man had started to climb the hill again. You stood for a while gazing at the sea, then climbed into the car.

—The old man knew my father. They often met below on that coastal track.

The sea, already made inaccessible by mangroves and bush-clad cliffs, receded in the background as we drove farther into the hills. Now we followed a quiet river which gleamed below a rocky plateau. We passed several stiff escarpments. Gradually the hills assembled and rose higher. They drew farther from us, and rain clouds began to swathe their blue-black sides.

The afternoon sulked in the highlands. It had rained heavily in the hills. The road was sluggish. We inched slowly uphill. We heard the turbulence of the river behind clumps of bamboo. Occasionally, above the sound of the water, came a shrill cry from a Fijian village.

A rough wind followed us through the thin-scalped, terraced hills.

Soon we were descending into grazing land where the air reeked of cattle dung. The river reappeared. We met squalls of rain on the low hills and along the river. Now our thoughts were full of the city of rain.

The city was in a storm. The electric power had failed. Water gushed in the streets. There was no traffic on the road. The houses were closely shuttered and braced to face the wind. You dropped me at my apartment. The car swung around, the headlights full on my face. It shot away in the dark with the tail light blinking.

From my bedroom I heard the car speeding out of the city. There were whorls of light in the city's outlands. I sat in its glow feeling lost again. I didn't know then that I wouldn't see you for a long time.

I phoned the hospital several times. There were contradictory answers to my enquiries. No one knew your whereabouts. You had apparently moved. There was no call or postcard from you. I searched for you like a madman feeling angry and helpless. Finally I learned you had gone to Australia, and from there proceeded to the United States with Moina.

I stayed inside the apartment till the green carpet and the bed clothes started to reek with my body odors. I had those nightmares again of startled birds falling about me into a slough.

It rained like the night we had returned to the city. I needed medicine. I put on a raincoat over my sleeping clothes and stepped on the wet stairs. Next instant I was in the mud below. The stairs blurred before me. I felt a sour taste in my throat.

A road worker saw me crawling in the mud. He took me to the hospital in a taxi. I slept fitfully on the hospital bed, and saw the haunting stream, a band of darkness between faintly illuminated foliage, and a corpse wrapped in a white sheet floating between the fearful ivi trees. I dozed off. I woke up in the morning thinking of the lonely executioner in the abandoned house. I felt rested and happy.

I saw you again a year later at a fair in Albert Park. You were with Moina. You both had changed. You wore glasses, and there was a lost look about you. Moina had cut her hair which gave her a boyish appearance. Moina saw me. I shall never forget the expression on her face—a mixture of fear and desperation. She reached toward you with sudden fierceness, and clasped your arm. You saw her fallen face, and looked over your shoulder. Till this day I haven't been able to decide whether you saw me or not. Next instant Moina steered you into the crowd.

Karma in My Psyche

—Where have you been, Anandi? Where do you always hide? Mother wailed.

I came out of my hiding place rubbing my nose.

—Oh, so the boy has tantrums. She tried to hold my hand, but my thin limbs stiffened.

She raised her eyes to the ceiling and sobbed. She cursed my brother Basu who had secretly married a Muslim woman, found a job with a merchant who owned stalls in the market, and moved to the outskirts of town. Basu's great dream was to have a job and live in town. Mother went to town to wage war on Basu and his wife. To keep Mother away, Basu sent her money every Friday.

Mother's attention turned to Mewa Lal, my father. She heaped abuse on him for dying just like that, leaving her stranded without a man's support. Mewa Lal's demise changed my status. An ailing middle child, I had slipped unnoticed into a family of three girls and an elder brother. I was taken care of by Ganga, a mid-wife with a mustache and a soldier's voice. Years later, when Mother died, she came to town in her enormous black skirt to claim me.

—You're an orphan now, she said in her coarse male voice, clucking her tongue.

Greatly moved by this gesture, I retained her as a housekeeper until Gaytri, my wife, dismissed her for prying into our wardrobe.

After Mewa Lal's death, Mother started taking notice of me.

—Come to me, Anandi, my householder, she said, drying her tears and feigning cheerfulness.

She made little ditties for me.

—What will Anandi be when he's a man? Will he be a doctor and take care of his Mother? He'll be a taximan, and take his mother on a long journey.

Mother noticed that although my legs were quite hollow, the paws were extraordinarily large. She stared at them.

—Why are your feet so big, Anandi? They're almost as large as Masiha's!

I stretched my legs irritably, and examined my feet. They were lanky and awkward. They didn't seem to be my own feet. Mother kept me indoors, and told me exemplary tales about pious and dutiful sons.

Masiha was my grandfather. One of his photographs shows him sitting on a wooden chair in front of a large thatched house. He is wearing a black coat over his dhoti. His turbaned head is unnaturally erect. But there is a raffish grin on his lips. Grandfather's extraordinary presence in the photograph is somewhat diminished by the great effect of the bright and bare yard. I believe that it was in that brooding, mud-plastered yard, drenched in mid-morning tedium, that Grandfather discovered the devil and the holy man in him, and made his pact with Satan.

After eating his treacle, the old man invited me on his knee. I leaned against his wide chest, and heard him grinding his teeth, making a clattering sound. He told me about his horses. When he was a young man, in another country, he rode Turkoman horses, thirty-ribbed and sixteen hands high. The horses were distinguished by their white feet and a blaze on their foreheads. They were bred in a princely state from horses that pulled the chariots in the Indian epics. Grandfather's horses were called Tartar and Chandu and Shaan.

Years later, in a high school history book, I read that the chariots were often driven by wild mules.

When the sun was high up, Grandfather went into his garden behind the house to survey his lime trees. I trotted at his side. We plodded up a rocky hill, the old man puffing and clicking his teeth. I sat on a flat boulder under a casuarina tree. The old man ruffled my hair and wheezed from phlegm-filled lungs.

At the bottom of the hill, Babari Ban drowsed in the hot sun. A small creek with three muddy pools, where the children bathed during rainy season, divided the village and the bush. The village consisted of a dozen thatched houses, each with a small mud-plastered yard, on the two sides of a dusty track. Another group of houses straddled the side of a low hill. They belonged to Governor, the village sirdar. The bush began scantily at the creek, growing dense toward the western hills. The children ventured only into the edges of the thicker part of the bush for wild berries and passion fruit; the rest of the bush remained dark and mysterious.

I squinted at Grandfather's sturdy appearance as we climbed down. He was indeed a rider of horses. According to him, everyone in Barbari Ban was a cane cutter or a drain digger; mere peasants. But he was different: he was an adventurer. He told me about his adventures in the far corners of the island. Sometimes he went alone, sometimes with other wayfarers. It seemed that the unpeopled jungles of the island brought out all his wayward energy. He even ventured into Jahanuum, a district notorious for its bushmen, thugs, and slave dealers.

From one of his adventures he returned with a girl of twelve. She was a mere apparition, thin-limbed and under-nourished. Her people had turned into bushmen and disappeared into the hills. She was too frail to follow them. She wandered from one house to another in her rags. She could neither cook food nor hoe in the sugar-cane field. Grandfather had to teach her to wash her body and cover herself properly. He made her his wife.

My little grandmother had two assets: a deeply husky voice and a ridiculously jealous nature. With the first she lured Grandfather, and they produced a team of eleven children. The second caused her to follow Grandfather about like a pariah, to the gin houses and jahajis get-togethers. She also had a loose tongue. She was foul-mouthed without shame. She embarrassed Grandfather wherever she followed him. He was filled with great revulsion and rage but he couldn't get rid of her: the adventurer was truly trapped.

One day a stranger arrived in the village. No one knew where he came from. He had a tiny mustache on a stony face, wore a tattered raincoat, and smoked a sweet-smelling cheroot. The children called him "Barsati" because of his raincoat, which he never took off. The villagers hurrying toward the sugar mill in the chilly morning greeted him suspiciously as he walked purposefully, without skulking, toward the village. The dogs didn't trouble him. They yelped a couple of times, and followed him timidly as he prowled in the village, playing with the children and chatting pleasantly with the women.

In the evening he weaved his way to the rum shop, and bought everyone a drink. He told tall stories and everyone laughed, and he bought more drinks. Grandfather was slumped in a corner of the rum shop. He had escaped from Grandmother by chaining her ankles and tying her to a bedpost. When he was fully drunk, he took Barsati aside.

A quiet transaction took place between them. Grandfather invited him to stay the night with him.

There was a hysterical crying in Grandfather's house early in the morning. And then there was silence. The following day Barsati was no longer seen in the village. Three village women, including Grandmother, had disappeared. The villagers realized what had happened when Grandfather bragged at the rum shop that he had sold Grandmother for five pounds. Barsati turned out to be a recruiting agent for a coconut estate on a faraway island.

Soon after this incident an epidemic of marsh flu broke out. It killed many women and children in Babari Ban and the neighboring villages. Grandfather believed he had done Grandmother a favor. The wretched woman would have surely died, he told my father Mewa Lal.

Some years later, Grandfather crossed the sea to Taveuni with a consignment of stolen New Year's goats. He arrived on the island in the evening, and managed to find shelter for the night in the workers' barracks of a copra plantation.

Grandfather was tired. He found a comfortable corner to sleep in after polishing off the left-overs in the smelly kitchen. His host was a garrulous man. Grandfather could hardly bear his palaver. The man told him about Mr. Ackroyd, the lonely bed-ridden part-European planter, who had died two years before leaving all his property to Mrs. Ackroyd. The story puzzled Grandfather in the morning. There were details about the story he wanted to remember but couldn't.

After he had dispatched the goats, Grandfather decided to look the place over, and perhaps catch a glimpse of the lucky Mrs. Ackroyd. He did his ablutions in a stream, and no sooner had he crossed the bridge toward the hill-top bungalow when his eyes fell on a woman walking out of the back door into the garden. She wore a blue frock, and had curlers in her hair. Grandfather had experienced numerous unexpected encounters in his life, but the devil himself wouldn't have drawn the crestfallen expression he suddenly wore when he saw Grandmother. He made a quick about face, hurried to the wharf, and stepped aboard a waiting steamer. He left the island posthaste without looking back.

Something happened to Grandfather when I was six years old. He seemed like a tired war horse. He seldom ventured out of Babari Ban. One by one all his sons went over to Mrs. Ackroyd. Only Mewa Lal remained loyal to him. One day he summoned Mewa Lal to him, and told him he was handing over the house and all his belongings to him and his wife and children. He himself was going to build a hut on the other side of the creek at the edge of the bush. Mewa Lal begged him to stay with him. But the old man had made up his mind. He continued to come to see me, and eat his treacle. Sometimes he attended the epic recitals at Governor's bure.

Suddenly he disappeared without telling anyone. The villagers said he had gone into the bush and become a sanyasi.

It is quite possible that Grandfather really wanted to do something saintly. After some months he returned to Babari Ban with a new faith. He called himself a Presbyter. He wore a flowing saffron-colored robe. His long hair fell lankly in curls over his shoulder. He gathered the children who didn't attend school, or were too little, and herded them to the creek where they bathed and sang hymns. The children's mothers were quite happy to have them out of their way. In fact, they actively encouraged their children to follow the others to the creek.

An odd ritual took place at the creek. While the children sang the hymns, Grandfather had his favorite pupil knocked into the creek. He was pushed down under the water until he choked and cried out. If he endured the test, he was given a new name—Emmanuel or Nathaniel. This was Grandfather's way of instructing his followers about survival. From the creek they marched to the hut where he preached about the end of the world. He predicted there would be a series of fires followed by a huge conflagration, and after that a great stampede toward the sea. Only those who were able to swim would survive.

I didn't become a Presbyter. By now I was already attending a small school by the sugar mill. The old man left me alone.

An alien sect was taking root in Babari Ban. The villagers were alarmed. Someone saw Grandfather talking to a white priest in town. It was reported at the mandali recital. Then the rumors began that Grandfather was feeding his followers buffalo meat. Now the villagers were enraged. Some of the elders called on Governor to arrange a meeting of the whole village.

It was a historical meeting, held in the Governor's palaver house, an open bure, a few chains away from the group of houses in which Governor and his family lived.

Governor was held in great esteem because he was a sirdar. But he was also very knowledgeable. He had traveled to Viti Levu. He had a large, unmanageable family scattered all over the islands. There was always a new face at Governor's house, a distant relative who came for a favor, or just to sleep for the night. The only other person who commanded such respect was Mr. Nambiar. He was admired more secretly by those who liked his progressive ideas. But most people preferred to keep away from him because he had been a leper, and had spent ten years at Dalice Bay.

On the night of the meeting, the villagers marched eagerly to Governor's palaver house with their families. Governor sat on a bench with three other elders. The women huddled together on one side. I found a vacant space between the little Presbyters who sat with their heads bowed. We watched Damodaran, Governor's niggardly son, snarling orders to the lads who were hurrying around with bowls of red tea and yaqona. He was always in the wings, watching his father roll his cigarette. Governor picked the tobacco with two fingers from a gold tin, lit his cigarette, pulled it with a sucking noise, and, throwing his head back, he blew the smoke through his nostrils.

Governor rose to his feet, placing his hat on the bench. He described how hard this kind of meeting was, and how he wished the Panchayat still existed to take care of such matters. He stuck the dead cigarette over his ear. His tone changed as he came to the main point of his speech.

—We have lived together in this basti for over thirty years. While others went to the big river toward the heart of the island, we stuck to this place. Everyone said it was no place to start a life. We made it into something. We have maintained a peaceful life. We have had our feuds. Every family has feuds. But we have remained united. My family is all over the islands. When my mother died, we all came together. We were united in our sorrow and need. We are like that in this village.

—We are a Hindu community. We have inherited our ways which have a long and ancient history. We have our festivals, and we meet every week for Ramayan recitals. We don't influence other people's beliefs, nor do we put pressure on our own people. In that way, our faith is the truest faith in the world.

He paused.

—That doesn't mean we shouldn't safeguard our way of life. Now I come to something disturbing that is happening in Babari Ban. We find a strange sect growing in our midst whose practices are against our own beliefs. We would have ignored it. But our very own children are being led astray. We cannot turn a blind eye any more.

The speech had a remarkable effect. It was remembered for a long time. Everyone wanted to hear more. But the three old men on the bench were becoming visibly impatient. After his speech Governor introduced them, and asked how the village could deal with this problem.

—Jolai must conduct the religious ceremonies more strictly; he has gone too far away from the ancient books, grunted one old man.

Jolai, the pundit, reeled back and snorted, as if he were being kicked in his soul. He let out a half-croak, and turned his eyes in Governor's direction for support.

—The women must maintain their fasting. They avoid salt on fast days, but gorge themselves with sweets. They've become slothful in their ways and can't control their children, harangued another old man. A couple of younger women giggled discreetly.

There were many agitated voices now.

—But first we must do something about the Byters, someone shouted from outside the bure.

—We must give the tottering messiah and his buffalo-eaters a muddy bath.

These were the voices of the cane cutters who had arrived late. They stood outside in the dark, smoked, and talked among themselves to express their displeasure at this beating about the bush.

Several people had started to talk at once. The tiny Presbyters tittered nervously.

Governor's voice rose above the din. The Presbyters hung their heads timidly. Then Governor uttered a word which revolutionized the political life at Babari Ban—"Committee." It created a new caste of Committee men. Smart and spruced, these men met secretly at various places, and spent long hours away from their farms and families to debate the weighty affairs of Babari Ban.

Babari Ban's first Committee was entrusted with the business of inventing ways to combat the conspiring Presbyters. But the Committee temporarily forgot Grandfather's messianic maneuvers when the weekly cane fires started. Governor was the first victim. Within a month every villager suffered from these fires. The Committee quickly transformed itself into a vigilante group, and created its own anarchy: a woman who had stolen to the creek for an amorous adventure was molested, apparently by a Committee man, and a mill shift worker was beaten up, also by a Committee man.

Grandfather was no longer seen in the village. The cane fires stopped temporarily. Grandfather's bewildered followers were left in total disarray. They toddled up to the master's hut, sat around or played, and returned to their homes at mid-day.

Finding the right anarchic moment, the arsonist struck again. The vigilantes saw someone like the wild Presbyter himself whooping and hooting by a burning cane field. The pelted him with stones, but he disappeared into the bush. His hut was razed to the ground. Once in the bush, he became fair game. The vigilantes hunted him down. It is possible that Grandfather had played out his game, and had grown tired. He wanted to be caught. At the end of the week, the vigilantes brought him from the bush with a noose around his neck. They hoisted him up a high pole and cross-tied him. That is how he acquired the name Masiha.

Some mill workers saw Masiha hanging from the pole early in the morning. Before the women and children were out of their houses, the Committee men dug a hole in the bush and buried him.

Babari Ban had become used to Grandfather's migratory behavior. He wasn't missed for a long time. Mewa Lal told us that Grandfather would return to Babari Ban one day, after he was tired of his adventures. I knew he didn't believe that.

I watched Mewa Lal, my father, pedaling his Hercules toward the village. Past the creek, past Mr. Nambiar's house, the bicycle lurched down the rutted lane, the tiny silver bell creating a great racket. The bicycle cruised onto the broad village path. Mewa Lal whistled and smiled at everyone. The children squealed and raced behind him.

I rode with Mewa Lal to the mill ground for a football match on a Saturday afternoon. I was perched on the handlebars. My father smelled pleasantly of Ingram's shaving cream. At the match, he shouted and cheered like a child. I ate watermelon, and watched a train take trucks of sugar cane to the mill. After the football match, we stopped at the tennis court where four players in white uniforms were performing a ritual dance in the fading light.

On Sunday Mewa Lal overhauled his bicycle. His fingers and the sleeves of his shirt were covered with grease. He looked like a mechanic. Some Sundays a barber came over to cut his hair and give him a shave. He sat on Grandfather's chair in the yard, wrapped in a white apron. The barber hovered around him. They talked about movies that neither of them had seen. All Sunday Mewa Lal smelled of freshly cut hair and shaving cream.

Mewa Lal started his career as a stable boy. Grandfather called him "my stable-boy son." He looked after the horses at the mill stable. Sometimes he escorted the horses to the sugar mill for Mr. Wile and Mr. Steer, who were field overseers, to ride to work.

I had persuaded Grandfather once to take me to the stable to see the horses. Perched on a wooden fence, we watched a man shoveling manure and stirring a lot of dust. The horses neighed and jumped toward the fence.

—They aren't real horses, Grandfather said derisively. He called them "weedy sons of horses."

Mewa Lal appeared with a bucket and rags to wash the horses. He cleaned their tapering heads, from the eyes and ears to the muzzle, then their withers and rounded croup and haunches. We waited till he adjusted the riding pad and saddle, and started to walk the horses toward the sugar mill.

Grandfather mocked his son's servile manners. But the mill officers were pleased with his underdog's dutiful smile. Mewa Lal was soon taken off stable duties and was promoted to the position of a messenger-mailman and part-time telephone operator at the mill exchange. Now he parted his hair and sported a mustache, and rode a green Hercules. We were pleased with the bicycle, but greatly embarrassed by the way he rode it, like a boy scout, making all the signals to the great amusement of bystanders, whether he was in a busy town or a lonely village lane.

Mewa Lal developed a late interest in Bombay movies. Every Saturday night he rode to the cinema. Nothing deterred him, neither a storm nor sickness in the family. When mother reminded him about the mandali recitals, Mewa Lal replied that the movie was about the life of Rama.

—Next thing you'll find the bicycle at a gin place.

Mother eyed him coldly all Sunday. She was convinced the movies caused men to be lured to unchaste women and drunkenness. She never allowed us to go the pictures. She granted Mewa Lal this extravagance because he was otherwise of frugal habits, and as a working man, he was entitled to a single foible. He brought us blue and pink handbills. We stuck them on the windows and gazed at the great Rajpilt dueling and romancing on horseback. Mewa Lal rode his bicycle singing:

Beloved
You and I
One of these days . . .

I have sometimes asked myself: was Mewa Lal a happy man? It seemed that he had decided long ago that there was a hidden hand behind everything. It was enough that he should do his duty and maintain a cheerful disposition.

My father was the most unexcitable man in all of Babari Ban.

One wet night the hidden hand struck Mewa Lal. After a Saturday night movie his bicycle swerved from a footbridge straight onto a sleeping horse. The horse gave a startled kick that sent both man and bicycle trundling into a filthy sewer. When Mewa Lal didn't return well after midnight, Mother organized a search party. We found him half buried in a soggy ditch still holding on to his bicycle. He remained in a stunned condition all week. But soon he was himself again.

He died quietly on a Sunday after a hair cut and chat with the barber about the latest movie extravaganza. Throughout the morning of the funeral, I leaned against the wall staring at my father's bicycle. Several women came and hugged me and burst into tears. Basu looked around nervously for me. I was strangely comforted by Governor's presence. He sat on Grandfather's chair rolling his cigarette. They called me when Mewa Lal's body was being washed for burial. I didn't want to touch him, feeling distressed by the way everyone gazed at his dead body. I followed Basu and three other men who carried my father to the hill. I hid behind a casuarina tree, and watched his body being lowered into the grave. I pressed my bare feet on the prickly casuarina seeds, feeling hot tears rolling down my cheeks.

At the age of ten, I found myself wedged between Mewa Lal's self-ease and Grandfather's heroic fantasies. I also had something of Mother's great capacity for unhappiness.

School saved me from Mother. I got ready for school before the cry of any slothful rooster. I put on my baggy shorts and a shirt that was a size too large: Mother expected me to finish school in that uniform. I hurried away from home with a bag crammed with books dangling against my bony side. In school I was regarded as a determined learner; I won prizes for regular attendance and for intoning a psalm.

I started to take on adult manners. I furrowed my forehead and I hung my lips like a grown-up.

When it was raining continuously, I experienced a sense of panic watching the earthworms coming out from the damp corners of the house. I ran to the neighbor's house to listen to their Marconi. The inside of their house was clean and dry; the beds had soft cushions and colorful mats. In the kitchen there were rows of glasses and cups that no one used. I admired this family. It was a real family. It had men who worked in the farm or the sugar mill, and women who milked the cows and planted rice, and fed the children. They gave me tea and boiled peanuts, and talked about my adult ways.

Mother strutted in the yard and gritted her teeth at these women who had lured me away.

Sometimes I went for long solitary walks.

—Only the devil walks like that. Talking to yourself all the time . . . Mother sighed.

She decided it was time she took me to Jolai. The bonesetter-astrologer-dentist-quack was perched on his haunches like a wizened toad, nursing a queazy stomach.

—The boy's causing a lot of trouble, Baba, Mother lied.

Jolai made a croaking sound and swung his head from side to side, working his sagging mouth. Mother frowned at the brushing-away movement of his hand.

—The boy's talking to himself all the time, Punditji. Living in his own world. I think he's trespassed something sacred, Mother prodded him.

Jolai held me with his eyes, and then let me off. He crawled to the door to spit. He wiped his lips gazing stolidly at my face for a while. He reached for an oil-smeared bundle on a grimy ledge. He opened the bundle and brought out a mildewed volume. Mother shifted close to me, pleased that Jolai was considering a full reading. Jolai turned the molding pages, and paused at a page written in the zodiacal alphabet. He snatched my hand abruptly and bent close to me. His trousers gave off the odor of unwashed genitals. He ran a wrinkled finger over the crisscross of lines from my little finger up to the heart line, stopped where the line curved upward, and followed it with his eyes till it faded into a loop. He flicked his tongue, and turned to a page full of arcane words. Still holding my hand he tilted his withered head to study the line from another angle.

His reading was interrupted by the call of nature. He hobbled outside. When he returned, he went straight into another room. We waited patiently. His head, splattered with sandalwood paste, popped out. He called Mother aside apparently to disclose his findings. He rooted two pellets from deep inside his trousers and placed them on Mother's hand with stern instructions.

Mother steered me outside. Jolai came to the door and spat on the ground. On reaching home, Mother flopped on the floor. She fanned herself vigorously with the end of her orhini and sniveled. She seized my hand just as Jolai had done. After a while she dropped it loosely. My sisters gathered around me.

—What did Jolai say, Ma, they chorused.

Mother rubbed her swollen leg without saying a thing. She smiled to herself, consoled by some secret understanding.

In bed at night, I heard my sisters whisper,

—What did Jolai tell Ma?

—Anandi has trespassed something really bad.

—Ma, says Anandi, is a blackguard.

—What does that mean?

—I don't know. Ma says Anandi's seventh house is empty.

That night my dream of the black swamp returned. The solitary pandanus stood like a ghost. I was crouched among tall reeds. A flock of birds swooped from behind me, deafening me with the violent swish of their wings and wild clacking of beaks. I ran toward a group of men working on a railway line, a cry that was like my mother's pursuing me. I heard the chug chug of a train. I cried for help but no one heard me.

When my eyes opened, I found myself struggling with the bolt in the back door, still in my dream, running from my invisible pursuer.

The following morning Mother nailed a horseshoe on the back of the door.

Mansa Ram wasn't my friend. We only walked to school together. The boy had pimple scars all over his face. This made him seem older than he was. It was difficult to tell his real age. He also had a bad stammer.

Mansa Ram hated school, didn't care for reading and writing. Once or twice a week he would spring up behind me like a thief, begging me to compose a letter to his teacher. At first he provided the story, I simply embroidered it. He wasn't easily satisfied. Although the stories he gave me were absurdly melodramatic, he wanted the account to be realistic and moving. I ceased to depend on Mansa Ram's stories, and spent a great deal of time inventing new incidents that happened to my unfortunate hero which prevented him from attending school. When Mansa Ram was satisfied, he grinned and handed me two pennies to spend at Ming's shop. He always had money in his pocket. His father had a stall in the market. He also made a lot of money from organizing games at various fairs.

I scrambled off to school with Mansa Ram's epistle, while Mansa Ram swaggered aimlessly in search of adventure. He was greatly fascinated by anything that was mobile, and would jump onto a moving trailer or lorry with the greatest ease. Sometimes I wondered why he was so free, and I so tied to the ground.

I shared Mansa Ram's dislike of teachers. They barked and snarled in shrill voices, and harbored subtle hostilities among themselves. They tossed chalks at us in anger, or pulled our ears. When the new Headmaster, Mr. Knowland, a disciple of Gandhi's non-violence, removed corporal punishment, the teachers implemented a new method of punishment: they made us slap our own faces. It was invented by a Brahmin arithmetic master who had great fear of pollution. But we preferred to be punished by the teachers because in our endeavor to render a convincing punishment on our own faces, we often hurt ourselves considerably more than we deserved. One boy, Ram Kissun, a crooner with a girlish smile, literally leveled himself to the floor. The Brahmin master, unconcerned, smiled while Ram Kussin struggled to his feet with a foolish grin on his face.

I was made to slap my face for day-dreaming in an arithmetic class.

Only Azad, the handsome Muslim boy, didn't suffer any of these indignities. I wanted to be his friend. He had elegant manners. His father brought him and his two sisters to school in a small black car. The girls were fair, and wore starched frocks. Azad was always reading interesting books. He said he wanted to be a doctor. We never became friends.

The teachers didn't tolerate laughter very much. One morning we were trooped in front of the school building for prayer. The deputy Headmaster called us to attention. The pre-assembly hubbub died as soon as Mr. Knowland appeared. Mereoni, the big Fijian girl from our class, kept on giggling. She had to stay back after school to write a hundred times that she wouldn't laugh in the assembly. At the following morning's assembly we prayed for Mereoni. But Mereoni wasn't there. She never returned to school.

The class was dull without Mereoni's laughter. But the class livened up when Mr. Rainey, our new class teacher, arrived. We all liked Mr. Rainey. He was very gentle, and he listened to everyone patiently, and spoke to us without condescension. He corrected our notebooks without making angry marks. Some boys had scabies. He examined their hands, and had them washed and treated. I did everything perfectly for Mr. Rainey.

Late in the year I fractured my arm while playing football in the rain. I missed a whole week of school. My hand was cast in a tumeric plaster and I stayed in bed.

The day was hot. Some children were blowing whiffs of chicken feathers in the air. At the back of the house, a woman was crooning a mournful song. Mother went on with the house work, glad that I was in the house. She found some excuse to come to my bed, saw my angry face, and turned away.

Suddenly the children stopped playing. I heard Mr. Rainey's Austin turn onto the village road. The children stared at the tall figure in white shirt and shorts marching toward our house, as if he had come to the wrong place. Mr. Rainey greeted Mother in Hindi. Mother stood at the door holding her orhini over her mouth. Mr. Rainey came straight to my bed. He had fruits for me in a brown paper bag. He sat on the edge of the bed and examined my arm, and told me anecdotes about our class. We laughed together.

Heads straggled at the two windows, and eyes peered through the cracks in the wall.

Before Mr. Rainey got into his car, he stood in front of the large flaming bougainvillea tree, admiring the flowers which were turning purple in the hot sun. I slouched in the doorway, and wished Mother hadn't swept all the rubbish under the bougainvillea.

I said to Mansa Ram that we should invite Mr. Rainey and show him our village. Mansa Ram wasn't impressed with the idea.

—There's nothing to show in Babari Ban, he said, hunching his shoulder.

I realized how right he was. There were no landmarks in the village, nothing to hold anyone's feelings or imagination, only the faceless hills and bush. All that was wonderful was elsewhere or in books.

Mother's attitude toward me changed perceptibly. I heard her telling the neighbors that Mr. Rainey was taking me abroad, and that I would soon become a doctor. I demanded that she stop telling these lies. Mother went ahead preparing me for my studies by putting me on her oil treatment. She fed me fish oil to fatten me, rubbed coconut oil on my head to keep it cool, and made me swallow great quantities of castor oil to clean up my inside. She waited for me in Ming's shop to take me home after school. I saw her sitting in Ming's shop front shelling peanuts. I slipped away through the back. At home I threatened to run away if she embarrassed me any more by coming to the school.

At night I did my school work under her gaze. I lay on my stomach copying notes from a textbook. The mud floor was cool on my stomach. Mother shifted the lamp close to me and crouched beside me, smiling with satisfaction at the writing in my notebook. She folded her legs, and started to turn the pages of my exercise books. She moistened her thumb with her tongue and separated the pages with both her hands, blowing between the pages.

Mother had the enviable quality of never surrendering easily.

I felt irritated. I wanted to hurt her. I saw her bring her hand over her mouth and yawn. I raised my head, propped my chin on my hands, and cleared my throat.

—Ma, Mr. Rainey wants to know your name. I have to fill in a form. They can't find my birth certificate.

No one in Babari Ban knew Mother's name. No one dared to ask her. To everyone she was Anandi's mother. Sometimes in my anger I had asked myself who was this woman who pressed her suzerainty so stubbornly over me—and I didn't even know her name.

I expected her to explode with anger. Instead she went on turning the pages, looking down and smiling to herself. The girls who were playing with pebbles, tossing them off the backs of their hands and catching them in their palms, turned their faces toward us.

—Yes, Ma, what is your name? they chimed.

She started to scratch a mark on the floor without looking at us. A coy smile softened her mouth. She rocked back and forth. We waited. Finally she said:

—Can you tell?

The girls teased her with many unlikely and ridiculous names. She rocked with laughter. When she gained control, she said:

—Silly children, my name is Genda.

The girls chortled. I started to laugh. Mother laughed heartily with us. She was named after a flower—Marigold. I grew slightly fond of her that night.

Suddenly Mansa Ram was full of Mr. Nambiar and his books.

Mr. Nambiar lived by himself in a wooden house by the creek. I often saw him reading a newspaper on his front porch. Mansa Ram said Mr. Nambiar had a whole trunk full of books. Sometimes Mansa Ram escaped from school and read Mr. Nambiar's novels. I didn't believe him. But Mansa Ram was really changing.

One afternoon, I fell in by Mr. Nambiar's side as he wheeled his bicycle down from Governor's house. He smiled at me and said he had been to see Governor about some labor trouble. Encouraged by his friendliness, I strode alongside him on the narrow track between the paddy fields. I always felt there was something attractive about Mr. Nambiar. He was tall and lean, and had a strong face with dark peering eyes. His pants flapped pleasantly as he pushed his bicycle with his clawed hand. He went on discussing labor problems as if I understood everything.

I liked Mr. Nambiar. He had a special way of talking about the simplest of things. I wanted to see his books, and hoped he would invite me to his house. I wandered by the paddy fields in the afternoon, waiting for him. Sometimes he was very late because he had meetings to attend. He was a labor organizer. One afternoon I asked him about his books. He seemed pleased. He asked me to come to his house on a Sunday.

I strolled to his house on a bright Sunday morning. He was sitting on a canvas chair on his porch reading a newspaper. He was the only man in the village who read newspapers. I liked the way he read his newspaper, smoking, and rubbing his forehead lightly with his fingers in a thoughtful manner.

He was happy to see me. He invited me inside. He opened the book trunk, riffled through the pages of a couple of books, and handed me a Hindi novel.

—It's Mansa Ram's favorite, he said, rising to his feet.

It was hard to believe that Mansa Ram had read the book. I was enthralled by its touch and smell. It had a garish cover and smelled of mothballs. I spent most of Sunday reading the novel. Mr. Nambiar gave me lemon juice in a silver vessel and some nuts to chew.

The following week, I went to his house again. Mr. Nambiar gave me a photo album to look at. It had several photographs of him taken when he was much younger. They were from Dalice Bay. In some of them he was standing between two women of mixed race, his hands on their shoulders.

My attention was drawn to a photograph of a ten year old girl taken at a beach. She was holding the hem of her dress and testing the water.

She had large almond-shaped eyes and an oval face. Her face was lit up with laughter.

—That's Maya, Mansa told me.

She attended a boarding school in Suva. Every month Mr. Nambiar sent her money. The leper woman he had married died at Dalice Bay.

I had my first glimpse of the sea from a train on a school picnic. There were no beaches, only rocks and mangroves. The sea seemed far away, deep and black. We picnicked by a stream.

On the train I kept seeing the laughing face of the girl in the photograph. I was half in love with her. She occupied my thoughts wherever I went. She was my helpmate, my ideal love. Her face and hair had the aroma of fresh marigolds.

Mr. Rainey found me a weekend job at the tennis court. I was a ball boy. I marched to the tennis court in the ball boy's blue and white uniform. Mother kept it clean, displaying it on the clothesline. But her hopes of seeing me advance in this career were soon dashed when I returned home without my uniform.

It was a hot afternoon. The grass on the courts browned right before my eyes. I had three courts to service because the second ball boy was absent. My head was in a daze. I heard an impatient cry from one of the players. My limbs could hardly move from exhaustion. Next instant I felt a stinging slap on my sweating face. Sparks flew inside my head. My eyes burned with perspiration. Through my tears I saw a player in white walking away from me. In my anger I turned toward the clubhouse. Women in dainty frocks were drinking tea and eating cakes. I opened the fly of my trousers, held my penis in my hand, and peed on the grass. The women turned their shocked faces away. I darted out through an opening in the high fence.

Mother glared at me, stunned, when I told her. She held her orhini over her mouth to stifle a scream. Then she let out a terrible wail, slapping my head and tearing my hair.

—Hai Ma, the boy has ruined us, she shrieked, shaking me violently.

The girls, who were at the door, gathered around her and chanted,

—Yes, Anandi, what will become of us?

—How will you be a doctor now? Mother whined.

—I'll be a taximan, I snapped back. And I will take you for a long ride.

When everyone was asleep, I took the lantern under the mosquito net and read Mr. Nambiar's novel till the flame winked and went out. Everything was still. A train whistled; it seemed to be from another country. I listened to the sighing of the casuarina trees. The thud in my chest increased. I stared at the night's grayness through the cracks in the bamboo wall. The foliage of the lime trees shook. The grayness vanished.

I said to myself if I cried now no one will ever hear.

I avoided Mr. Rainey at school. I saw him walking with quick short paces in the corridor. He stood apart in the assembly, his hands clasped together in front.

I returned from school feeling unhappy. Mother remained sullen and aloof. I wanted to do something conciliatory, but she didn't look at me. When I returned from school on Friday, she wasn't in the house. There was no one home. My sisters were collecting firewood on the other side of the creek. I searched for Mother in the back yard. I found her lying on her back under the big bougainvillea tree. I had never seen her like that. She had dozed off. She seemed so small and vulnerable. A fly crawled on her bare arm. More flies buzzed over the rubbish heap. I wanted to wake her, and take her away from there. Instead I set off at a run toward the creek. I sat on the footbridge above the murky water, thinking what if she should die one afternoon. What would become of us?

Too Long, the big oafish Chinese boy, jabbed me in the arm in the school corridor.

—Did you know Mr. Rainey's going?

—That's not true.

I tried to walk past him. Too Long was always fond of debating and scoring points. And he told dirty jokes.

—Mr. Rainey's in real trouble, that's why.

I had noticed something strange in the behavior of the teachers. They were hurrying toward each other, talking in a whisper. Mr. Rainey looked distraught, and Mr. Knowland was especially severe in assembly.

—Everyone knows why Mr. Rainey isn't married.

Too Long waited to be challenged. Finally he gave up and dashed away chuckling.

The day was warm and pale. I walked alone in the playground. It was deserted except for some girls who strolled in pairs on the basketball field. I felt angry and depressed.

The rumor continued throughout the term. At the end of the year, Mr. Rainey was transferred to a school in Suva. Our class organized a farewell. We collected money for a present. The girls made a garland. Ram Kissun sang a song, and Azad made a beautiful speech. He said Mr. Rainey was not only a teacher but also a real friend. I presented him with our gift of a pen.

The year I was finishing high school, Mansa Ram showed me a clipping from Mr. Nambiar's newspaper. It was about Mr. Rainey. I read the account a number of times. Mansa Ram stared at me without saying a word. I knew both of us believed in Mr. Rainey's innocence. He was terribly betrayed and trapped. I wished he wasn't departing in shame. He had said once that he wanted to live here all his life. But the place was no longer friendly toward him.

Soon after this incident, Mansa Ram came up to me and said he was thinking of leaving the village.

—I might try some enterprise in Suva, he said like a young man about to run off to sea.

I didn't take Mansa Ram's talk seriously. He was behaving too much like a character in Mr. Nambiar's novel.

The same week Mansa Ram disappeared from the village taking all his stepmother's jewelry with him.

—Mansa Ram . . . Mansa Ram. What will become of Mansa Ram, Mother chanted, staring at me from the corner of her eye.

Years later when I had finished my University studies, and started work at the Social Welfare, I received a card that at once surprised and thrilled me. It was from Mr. Rainey. There were two lines in his familiar handwriting. He congratulated me, and said he was writing with the pen I had presented to him. There was no return address on the card.

I went to visit Mr. Nambiar before leaving the village. He came out onto the porch, dropped the wad of papers he was carrying in his hand on the floor, and clasped my hand. He directed me to a chair, and sank in his own canvas chair, loosening his tie. Mr. Nambiar was now the leader of the labor union.

We sat there on his porch talking, with the afternoon sun shining on us.

—For the most part, our natural ability is all we have. The doors have opened for you, I'm so glad.

After a pause, he said:

—Sometimes I wonder what we are doing here. Babari Ban is so small. Mansa Ram left thinking like that. But this village needs its fame-makers.

He went on talking like that. I enjoyed Mr. Nambiar's special way of saying things. He always seemed to be looking at us from another world. From Dalice Bay. He said thoughtfully:

—Babari Ban is small. The world is so big. It's difficult when the scales start to fall from your eyes.

Smiling at me again, he said:

—What will you do, Anandi? After your scholarship, I mean.

I had only a vague sense of what I wanted to do. Something that would affect the whole world. I blushed after telling him that, because people in Mr. Nambiar's novels thought like that. But he seemed to understand. He nodded and said:

—There are many struggles, and everything works against us in so many ways. You'll have much time to think when you are studying.

I rose to leave. He walked across the yard with me.

—You're almost as tall as I am.

He gave a short laugh, and touched my bony sides.

—But you have to be strong. And light on your feet to do great things.

He laughed again. After a pause, he said:

—You are different, Anandi. You are not like Mansa Ram.

I walked home thinking about his last remark.

I met Gaytri a year after returning from my studies. I had started work at the Social Welfare. She was introduced to me at a wedding. I liked Gaytri. She was attractive, had traveled abroad, and had pleasant ways. She had attended a college in Australia for a couple of years, got lonely, and returned to her parents who owned a small shop in town. She wanted to work, but there was no urgent need because her parents had enough money, and she was the only daughter.

Gaytri called at my office unexpectedly one morning shortly after we met each other. We had lunch together in town. She invited me to meet her parents that weekend.

We were married that very year. It was precipitated by two factors: I was getting weary of my abstemious existence, and Gaytri, now past her mid-twenties, wanted a home of her own, to start a family life. Gaytri's parents were very pleased with me: I had a secure job and excellent prospects for the future.

I remember the wedding only vaguely. Gaytri had a great passion for weddings; she rarely missed a wedding invitation. She wanted a traditional Hindu wedding for us. She was draped in a glittering red sari, her face, hands, and feet covered in wedding make-up. For me she selected a three-piece suit instead of the traditional dhoti. After four rounds of the holy fire, I perspired and fainted, taking Gaytri down with me, the end of her sari being firmly knotted to a sash across my shoulders. The half-naked pundit, who until then was totally absorbed in his mantras, saw us falling, and lurched out of the mandup, hurling himself face down into a circle of panicking women. I was yanked away to the nuptial room.

When I opened my eyes, Gaytri was whimpering at my feet, still covered in a red veil. Gaytri's mother coaxed the pundit into concluding the nightmare wedding in the room.

Mother was convinced a mean influence was at work.

—It's Masiha, she told the distraught pundit.

She immediately prepared an offering of cooked rice, coconut, and incense and, as an after-thought, added some treacle. She arranged these carefully on a green banana leaf, and invited the pundit to hurl a few couplets.

I stole out into the cold night after Gaytri and the other women had dozed off in various corners of the room. I strolled down the empty street. A young man, one of my newly acquired relatives, came running breathlessly after me.

—Where's your home, I asked him, still walking.

He pointed to an unlit street behind rows of houses on stilts. I asked him to take me to his house. He made me some tea, after which I stretched out on a divan. I slept with the swarm of voices in the wedding tent and harmonium music buzzing in my head.

Gaytri gazed at me silently when I returned in the morning. She didn't seem happy at all. She had changed into an orange sari. Her face looked scrubbed and clean. Her mother brought me a breakfast of the previous night's puris and potato curry, and red tea. She stared at me while I ate as if I had done something unforgivably wrong.

Soon a yogi arrived with a bundle of herbs. Mother prepared a brew of boiled herbs in a huge black pot. I was taken to the back of the house. The yogi chanted incantations to the healing plants while Mother poured the brew down my head. My hair was a tangle of boiled herbs. I was driven to the sea in a taxi for a penitential dip.

The yogi prescribed total abstinence for a month. But Gaytri and I remained strangers beyond the thirty-one days.

And, as strangers, we moved into a half-complete concrete house at 70 Maravu Street in town. Gaytri seemed happy with the house. She prepared sweetmeats and tea for breakfast. In the evening I worked on my files, and Gaytri tried on her new clothes and jewelry. Sometimes she raised her hand, twisting her bracelets in front of me, saying:

—Aren't they pretty?

I raised my head and smiled. She wrinkled her nose and laughed coyly, her full sensual face glowing beautifully. She continued to look like a bride in her expensive clothes.

Gaytri slept in her sari on the bed. I spread a mat on the floor.

One morning Gaytri said:

—I feel so alone, Anandi, I don't feel at ease when you're away. The incomplete portion of the house seems so eerie.

—The landlord says he'll have the other section finished and give it out to a family. Then you won't be lonely.

—We could invite your mother to stay with us.

She expected me to be pleased.

I was alarmed.

—No, I protested. She'll not come here.

—But what is wrong with that? I will have company, and there's always so much to be done around the house.

Mother, who was growing tired of looking after her multiplying grandchildren, was greatly pleased that her daughter-in-law needed her. She arrived on the bus with her luggage.

Gaytri and Mother were drawn to each other like long lost sisters. They talked most of the night. Mother had lots of plans for the house. Gaytri listened to all her suggestions. In the morning they sat about re-organizing the house. One evening Gaytri announced to me that we were buying the house. Mr. Maharaj, our landlord, who had built the house from bits and pieces from a larger construction he was engaged in, had readily agreed to sell. In fact, Mother and Gaytri had already put a small deposit with him. Mother had convinced Gaytri that I was no good in these matters anyway. I did not quarrel. I wasn't especially thrilled with the house, but the prospect of having our own property did not displease me.

There was a lot to improve inside the house which kept Mother and Gaytri occupied. I spent more time away from home, sometimes with my colleague Raymond who invited me to his club in town.

One morning when I arrived back at the office after seeing a family, Raymond came into my office and said I should go home immediately. A neighbor had called. I was required urgently. I drove home straightaway. The front door of the house was ajar. I heard a whimpering sound in the bathroom. I froze at the bathroom door. Mother and Gaytri were on the floor like two unruly savages, and two hysterical women were trying to separate them. The sight was so ridiculous that I started to laugh. This brought the wrestlers apart. Mother got up wailing and cursing. Gaytri sulked on a heap of unwashed laundry.

Mother asked to be put on the bus that very afternoon. The following week Gaytri's mother arrived to set our house in order. She was a small plump woman who wore gold sovereigns to cure a goiterous growth. With her glasses and umbrella, she looked like a tiny professor. She announced through innumerable hints and innuendos that something awful and catastrophic had strayed into our house.

After I drove off to work, Gaytri and her mother set forth in search of Muni Baba, the man of many powers, an old indentured laborer who was reputed to possess the magical gandida tree. From it he had created the sraktya charm: a charm to compete with all charms. Muni Baba was a most elusive man. One day he was in one village, the next day he was in another. No one clearly knew of his whereabouts. But his preposterous cures were well known in the back reaches of our island. His fame had started to spread to Viti Levu. He was sought by great and small: politicians, policemen, football captains, gamblers, jealous housewives, hizras, bachelors, would-be headmasters, assassins, watermelon farmers, hospital orderlies, fire walkers, half-wits, and hypochondriacs. His medications ranged from such unusual elixirs as ashes raised from a dead man's entrails, cow piss, horse's milk, menstrual blood, to common oils and condiments. He accepted no gifts except gin or rum for the wayward deities, and a rooster for the more pagan ones.

Muni Baba was said to have admitted that his cures seldom reached perfection, not because he didn't have the powers, or that his clients lacked faith, but because in his world there were as many benevolent forces as there were subversive medicators. Nonetheless, for his faithfuls, whom the hospitals had failed, half a cure was preferable to none at all.

Muni Baba, like any good Brahmin, had great fear of pollution. That is why he never appeared before a client. He had to be contacted through a mediator. This go-between had access only to another go-between: Dwarka Nath, Muni Baba's loyal and beloved son. Of course this didn't mean that Muni Baba's presence wasn't real. In fact, the experience of his presence had become the subject of many legendary tales. A newspaper reporter described his encounter with Muni Baba's spirit in a crowded courtroom. Another time he was actually seen by the manager of a football team at a district match. Of course Muni Baba was wearing a disguise. The manager's team won the match.

After these visits to Muni Baba's village, Gaytri became increasingly self-absorbed. She was easily irritated when visitors came to the house. She complained of strange goings-on. One afternoon I found her plowing up the jasmine-scented front garden. Her eyes looked wild.

Before sleeping Gaytri sprinkled horse milk at the doors and windows. The dark unswept corners of the house began to bear a devilish melange of odors: gandhak, musil, and burnt offerings.

—The accumulated dunghill of a decrepit culture, I cried angrily one night.

Gaytri stared at me as if I harbored a dangerous sin. I started to observe her from a vast planetary distance: Gaytri was Manu's woman, full of wrath and impure thoughts, a lost life fluttering in the dark regions without a window to get out. There was nothing I could do except wait for the full play of her nightmares, and hope that one day they would all drain away.

I sought Raymond's advice at the office.

—Get drunk, he counseled me. Go home late. Create a scene. Break a few windows, and if she protests, use your hand.

Gaytri watched me coldly as I stamped about the house at midnight crying:

—I won't stand for this. I won't . . .

My voice was muffled by the flurry of rain against the windows.

However, this display seemed to have some effect on her. Gaytri led me to the couch. I held her hand and talked about the brevity of life. She nodded, saying,

—Yes, I know. My life, I understand.

We loved that night, and I slept peacefully every night that week thinking that I had triumphed at last. I thanked Raymond.

The following week Gaytri's own logic overturned the understanding of the previous week: I discovered an anointed string around her middle.

At first Gaytri resisted vehemently. She wouldn't hear of it.

—We'll have to ask Muni Baba first, she said.

—Why, isn't God's house free for us to visit?

—You have to believe these things, Anandi.

—I will go with you anyway.

We hired a taxi. The driver was a small ill-tempered man who drove the taxi during the day and sold cinema tickets at night. He kept repeating that he had to return to town before dusk. He drove recklessly, and we lost our way. We had to drive several miles back before we found the branch road leading to Muni Baba's village. The driver swerved the taxi onto a dusty lane, an old bullock-and-sledge track, with sugar cane on both sides. The track narrowed as we approached the village, and vanished into the yard.

Chickens squawked in alarm and fled behind houses.

The village was a semi-shanty settlement: box timber and old roofing iron nailed together to make small square shacks. Some had glass windows proclaiming that the village wasn't backward or unprogressive in any way. In the back, on a stretch of waste ground, were a couple of tumble-down grass huts, part of the old village.

One house stood apart: a wooden building painted in blue, its front cut in an Indian style. On the lower ground, at the edge of the sugar cane field, stood a small lavatory hidden by luxuriant banana leaves.

Gaytri walked quickly toward the house. I trudged behind her with two roosters, one black, the other red, in plastic bags. A young woman came out of the house clasping a baby and buttoning her blouse. She crouched beside an older woman who was washing dishes with soap and ash by an old water tank. I stopped a girl in a purple school uniform, and asked her if Muni Baba was at home. She stared at me with her large dark eyes as if she didn't understand.

We stood on the veranda gazing into the passage, waiting for a door to open. After some time a door opened a crack, then a little wider: someone was assessing me before making an appearance. Gaytri stepped into the front room cluttered with old and new furniture. A man appeared in the passage in undershirt and trousers. He wore rubber slippers on his oiled feet. He looked disappointingly plain, almost like a schoolboy.

Dwarka Nath peeked into each plastic bag and let out a scraping laugh. The black rooster was dead. Gaytri and Dwarka Nath gaped at each other. He glanced at me like a thieving mole, and led Gaytri into an inner room.

The pea-green wall of the front room had a row of photographs. I studied each photograph trying to find Muni Baba.

Gaytri returned for her purse. A glow of light showed when she opened the door to re-enter the inner room.

I lost interest in these proceedings, and strolled back to the car. Everything was so still before the light faded. The driver was chatting with some men who were drinking tea in an open shed. For a moment the village seemed such an attractive place: the workmen returning to the village and drinking their red tea, women coaxing wood fires, children playing in the dusk. But I hadn't come for this.

Gaytri came out of the house tying something to the end of her sari. On the way back I asked the driver,

—Have you seen Muni Baba?

The driver stared hard at me over his shoulder.

—There is no Muni Baba. Only a satanic imposter, I said, casually looking out the window.

Gaytri threw me a hostile glance.

—You haven't faith, Anandi. That is our undoing.

I was pleased with the way she called my name. I grinned at her. She smiled strangely and said:

—Did you not see how the black choked and died?

That week Mother died at the hospital. I didn't go to see her when she was taken ill. Raymond and I went to the village where she was buried in the hill next to Mewa Lal.

I started accompanying Raymond more frequently to his night club. We came out when the club was shut for the night. Then we drove into the back alleys, and ended up at some strange place where we had more drinks.

I complained of stomach cramps. The linings of my stomach were decomposing. Raymond believed that alcohol would make them immune to any foul play.

In a curious way, Gaytri seemed satisfied with my night wandering. Sometimes she seemed so much like Mother in the way she observed me, with that quiet smile. I am playing the game now, I said to myself. The monster is out in the open. Gaytri has something to fight. Gaytri met me at the door as I stumbled in. She knelt on the floor, opened my shirt, and pulled down my pants without once touching my body. Her breath felt warm on my navel. I stared down at her rich black hair. My body moved instinctively toward her, but a quick shove made me withdraw. She gathered my clothes, sprinkled them with tumeric water, and took them out in a bucket.

I staggered into the bathroom, and sat on the pan for a long time. When I came out, Gaytri was already asleep. Her black hair was coiled on the sheet like a serpent. She whimpered, and shifted farther to her side.

I returned from the office early one afternoon. Immediately I sensed there was something amiss as I entered the driveway. All the doors and windows of the house were open. There was a faint smell of jasmine coming from the bedroom. Gaytri was lying on the bed, her hair spread on the pillow, her mouth agape and her eyes shining from the bottom of some dark dream.

I moved frantically about the house, without feeling a thing, abusing Gaytri and cursing myself. I didn't know what I was looking for. I cursed the spell-binders as I examined Gaytri's purse and riffled through her notebook. I threw her things out of her drawers, cursing the joyless lot to which I belonged. I returned to the bedroom and thrust a wad of cotton wool into her mouth.

I knelt on the floor and looked under the bed. A little red bottle had rolled there. It was Gaytri's vial.

I watched her as she was prepared for burial. She was draped in a simple sari. She looked plain and conventional. That's what she really was. I realized more acutely now that what she had aspired for was so conventional. But she had been unlucky. All her props had started to fall on the wedding night, and she turned to the deceiving gods for help.

I had often seen Mr. Balmukund, my neighbor, a retired schoolmaster, taking the garbage out to the road. During the week of mourning, he came to the house with food in small silver containers. In the morning, he came back to collect his containers. He greeted me in the driveway when I returned from my morning walk.

Mrs. Balmukund seldom came out of the house. Sometimes she picked vegetables from the garden. She wore old faded saris with great care, which made her look younger than she was.

The couple lived in a small cream-colored house with a white fence. On weekends their two daughters, Deepa and Sushma, drove in with their husbands. The girls were as pretty as their names. Deepa had long slender arms and a lovely face. Sushma was taller and fairer, and she had long black hair. Their young men looked tall and slim in their narrow pants.

Deepa and Sushma drifted through the garden, turning from one plant to another, Mr. Balmukund closely behind them, his arms akimbo like a man about to perform a jig, so happy he was, drawing the girls' attention to a flower or a fern, guiding them on the stone path so that they would not soil their pretty shoes.

After the garden, the girls joined their mother in the kitchen. Mr. Balmukund entertained the young men in the front room.

I became a guest at their Saturday night dinner. Mrs. Balmukund spent the afternoon in the kitchen. She didn't want the girls to help. She just wanted them to be like the girls they once were. Mr. Balmukund advised the young men about building houses. Deepa and Sushma were about to have their own houses. He told us an often-told tale of seven brothers who started out in the depressed sugar cane field of Sigatoka. One of them worked his way to the teachers' college. The others were successful too. They remained farmers but they had their own concrete houses and their own families. It was the story of a hard-working successful family. It pleased us all. In the middle of his story Mr. Balmukund got up and peeked into the kitchen and said, Oh, it's Deepa doing the vegetables. He returned grinning like a man who had achieved everything.

At the dinner table, he tackled his food without taking his eyes off the plate. After he had finished, he smacked his lips, belched, and pushed his plate aside. The girls ate slowly, shyly urging their young men to take more food. Mrs. Balmukund made certain that I tried all the dishes. I felt a twinge of pleasure at her motherly concern.

We shared Mr. Balmukund's favorite whisky on Deepa's birthday. He was in great spirits. He gulped his first two drinks quickly and brought the glass down with a clatter, smiling at his wife. Mrs. Balmukund, now in charge of the evening, assumed a half-imploring, half-admonishing attitude, but she ended up being more generous than she intended, and poured him another large whisky. The girls giggled, waiting for the familiar family joke—Mr. Balmukund showing his affection openly toward his wife, calling her "K," a private code, ordering her to bring his old harmonium. With his wife by his side, he sang his songs, often forgetting the words, "K" providing the missing words and encouraging him to go on. The girls leaned on their husbands and tittered.

Later while Deepa and Sushma prattled in the kitchen, Mrs. Balmukund sat on the couch beside me.

—This is how we always wanted it, she said quietly. Nothing has changed. Deepa and Sushma are just as they were. Sailend and Victor are like our own children. There's such a thing as "apna-paraya," nothing changes that.

I turned my eyes to the girls, who came out of the kitchen and joined the young men on the settee. I thought how the two girls had fetched their husbands and returned to their family, and the young men, once outsiders, had broken the barrier of "us-and-them" and become children of this family. There was a moment of anxiety, Mrs. Balmukund told me, when both Deepa and Sushma fell hopelessly in love at the University. But in the end common sense won over love: the girls married these fine young men, from respectable families and with good civil service posts.

It was amid that sort of chatter that the inevitable happened: Shanta's name slipped out. The girls heard it and looked alarmed. There was a taut silence. Mr. Balmukund cleared his throat and looked away. Mrs. Balmukund took the cups and hurried into the kitchen.

The mystery that surrounded Shanta appealed to me greatly. It didn't take me long to put the pieces together and find her. I found her in a pleasantly-kept two-room apartment in town, by a kindergarten where she worked. She was draped in a white sari with a blue border. She was beautiful like Deepa and Sushma, but she also had a special attractiveness that emanated from her subdued but confident manner.

Shanta shared the apartment with Lorna. Lorna was with the Arts Council in Suva. Her husband David had an assignment with the Museum. She wanted to be away from Suva for a while, and since she had know Shanta at Auckland University, she arranged to stay with her.

I went to see them a couple of times. They were happy to see me. Lorna and I talked about the expatriate community in town. Shanta was usually quiet. On the weekend they invited me for dinner. We sat on the rug with our plates and listened to Shanta's records.

I was grateful to be with them, and began to dread nightfall and returning to the house with the wind whipping through the gulley.

One afternoon Lorna remarked:

—Your eyes have such a lovely brown. And they're so guileless. . . .

I saw Shanta staring at me from the corner of her eyes. She hurried away into the kitchen when she found I was looking at her.

After Lorna returned to Suva, Shanta started avoiding me. I didn't see her for some weeks. Later when I came to her apartment, she was preparing to go out. On the weekend her door was locked. One Sunday I parked my car outside her apartment, feeling the full desolation of the bright afternoon and radio music coming from the sleepy houses. Shanta returned just before the sun went down. How sad she seemed when she dropped her bag to open the door. I followed her inside, took her bag, and drew her to me and said I couldn't bear another weekend like this.

She wasn't altogether surprised. It seemed she half-expected me to act like that. She struggled at first and tried to pull away, and then came into my arms. I felt her tears on my face. She turned her dark, moist eyes toward me. There was real feeling in them. When I released her she withdrew into her room, and returned wearing a pink dress. We prepared dinner together.

—Why did you avoid me all these weeks, Shanta?

—What you're thinking about is impossible, Anandi. You don't even know me.

—I know enough about you to love you. I don't wish to know more.

—It's just because you are lonely you feel like that.

—I'm so happy when I think of you, Shanta.

After that, I went to see her every evening. Each time she showed a little more warmth and affection. She was changing.

For her birthday, I wanted to take her home.

—No, she insisted.

—Then let's go some place else away from here.

We took a bus to a rest house by the coast. We sat on the back seat holding hands. We spent the weekend by the sea, and were very happy for two whole days. I saw in her eyes that she wasn't going to be torn by grief anymore.

We married at the Registry.

The door of the cream-colored house closed forever for us. I had wanted so much to re-enter it with Shanta.

At first both Shanta and I were uneasy about setting up a household. Gradually we shed our self-consciousness. I followed Shanta about while she re-organized the house. She laughed at my behavior—a beau-

tiful, open laughter. She tilted her head, without looking at me, and said in Hindi:
—This is truly the end of me.
A lovely flush spread from her neck.
Now there was a closeness between us that felt like love.
When Shanta missed her periods I was terrified. I wanted her to be wrong.
—Are you sure? I asked her again.
After a month, she said,
—Something is eating my insides.
I was convinced she was imagining it. Little tapeworms, I told myself, eating their way out of tapeworm bellies.
We had a boy. Shanta gave up her kindergarten job. The following year we had another boy. I wasn't much good with the children. I let Shanta worry about their sneezes and chest colds. She spent much of her time keeping them clean. They clucked and gurgled in the bath, and touched her face and laughed. Shanta's hands started to have the dank smell of wet sheets.
As the boys grew older, they became sullen and egotistical, and clamored for Shanta's attention. She never lost her patience. She remained deft in everything she did.

The boys started school. During the end of the term holiday, I organized a picnic by the sea. They were so excited that they hardly slept the whole night. They woke up early to gather their picnic things. Shanta put on a lemon-green sari.
—Why are you wearing that, for heaven's sake, I cried impatiently, knowing well that she wouldn't touch the water.
We found a spot at the top of the beach under the shade of some evuevu shrubs. The boys chased each other in their bright swimming trunks. It was cool under the evuevu shade. I dropped my head on Shanta's lap and stretched out on the mat. Her fingers played nervously with my hair. Her eyes glanced up from my face and gazed at the sea. I closed my eyes and listened to the waves and the laughter in the distance.
The boys grew tired quickly and came back for their lemonade. I feigned sleep. Shanta attended to them without disturbing me. Her movements felt so pleasant. I opened my eyes to watch her moist face. The boys licked the red lemonade off their lips and stared at me. Their eyes said, Do you think this is fun? They dashed off in the sun again. I got up and walked down the beach wishing that Shanta and I could run

into the waves holding hands.

They boys held my hands and we strolled on the beach. We found some strange birds pecking in the mud. The boys were bursting with excitement, but they restrained themselves expertly. We knelt on the sand.

—There's a dead bird, they whispered, waving at Shanta.

I watched her walking toward us, her hair lifting in the wind. Her green sari gathered a lovely sheen in the sun. Her face glowed beautifully.

—What are the birds doing? the boys asked me, now less patient than in the beginning.

—They're carrying out a bird ritual, I replied. For their dead companion.

I looked up, searching for Shanta's face.

—They're burying the dead bird, they whispered to Shanta.

After the birds flew away, we collected our things, and started walking toward the car. I tried to keep the boys interested in the birds.

—Just imagine, I said. They flew all the way from Russia.

The boys were tired now and eager to get into the car. Shanta hurried to my side with a youthful motion, and took my hand.

She was awake for a long time. She turned toward me and touched my fingers, waiting for me to respond. I didn't because I was afraid, afraid that what she might say would upset the peace I had experienced with her. When I didn't say anything, she sighed and moved to her side.

The following morning she remained in bed. I took her a cup of tea. Her hands trembled as she took the tea, spilling it on her pink gown. I thought she would cry, but she didn't. Her face simply froze.

Later I said to her:

—You don't look well at all. You ought to take a break. Go away somewhere. I'll manage the boys.

Her face brightened. At last she found the opportunity to speak.

—Think about it, I said, avoiding her eyes.

I didn't really want her to go, and I was afraid of what she might say. In fact, I feared any new situation which might leave both of us desolate. She nodded quietly.

I drove to the town library. I had avoided this for a long time. Nervously I searched through a pile of newspapers, and found a bundle I wanted. Several issues were missing. Some had been scorched by the sun coming through the windows. Rainwater had got to others. But the particular issue I wanted was intact.

I had read the account of the fatal picnic the day after it occurred. The details had blurred in my mind. Now I read it again, and studied the photograph. The mountain pool was surrounded by jungle. An arrow pointed to the spot where Aziz's body was found. I re-read the story. It was all there: Shanta's background, her marriage to Aziz, a motor garage foreman and a Muslim who was married before, and the Balmukunds' rejection of Shanta. The rest of the story described the accident which happened barely a year after their marriage: Aziz swimming across to the waterfall, the noisy torrents of water cascading over the slippery rocks, the violent thrashing of limbs, and Shanta's panic.

She must have loved him deeply, I thought, as I drove back from the library. That is why she kept him where no one could touch him. In the seven years of our life together, I hadn't found a single token from him, neither a brooch nor a photograph with his signature.

Nothing happened the whole week. But I saw defiance building in her eyes. At the end of the week she received a letter from New Zealand. I found it on my working table. It was from Aziz's sister Jaitun. A flash of anger crossed my mind after I read its contents. So much had been taking place, yet I knew nothing. Shanta appeared in the doorway, drying the length of her hair with a towel. Even in my rage she seemed so beautiful and calm and innocent. Her expression changed when she saw the heat on my face. She withdrew into the bathroom.

I waited for her to mention the subject. When she didn't I thought she was vacillating, and perhaps even realized the folly of wanting to leave just like that.

Another letter arrived. I knew she had reached a decision. I could see she was prepared, and had a perfect hold on herself. I wanted to talk about the children, but I quickly saw the shabbiness of that argument. My thoughts were no longer clear. I was only aware of my need. I imagined her coming to me, her resolution melting, her smile reassuring me. But she did not raise her eyes.

I found myself surprisingly detached. I forgot my personal suffering and flung myself into the preparations Shanta had already started. She gathered her things. I helped with the children's clothes.

I drove them to the airport. When her flight was called, I pressed my face against her cheeks and tasted the hot tears. After a moment she disengaged herself, blowing her nose into a white handkerchief. She waved, smiling faintly, as she crossed the tarmac to the plane.

Some weeks later I received a letter from Jaitun. She apologized for not writing earlier. Shanta and the children had reached Auckland safely. Shanta had suffered an acute depression, but she was striving to be herself again. After a month Shanta wrote: I have a job at an Ashram, please don't laugh, it's not religious, I get paid. It's a bit like my job at the kindergarten. The boys are at a good school. Please don't worry about them. I'm very grateful for your understanding. I know deep down you saw how our feelings spoke against the life we were trying to create. As if nothing had happened. We have been impulsive. I know you will say we have been considerate, even loving, but only the way we are to strangers. I'm really happy to be starting out like this, and I'm sure in time your life too will find its own true course. Shanta.

After all these deaths and departures I was hardly ready for any further nest-mending. It was easier to think that life had simply passed me by, to feel like a voyeur, or a passenger on a train. I felt I was driven on in a great karmic space without arriving anywhere: my life had no center. But then I experienced that nagging assault in my guts. I couldn't simply abandon this life to the karmic will. I had to set my affairs in order which, in effect, meant removing myself from my post where life had reached an ignominious standstill, abandoning the nightmare house, and like a voyager deliberately missing a connection, breaking free of the karmic wheel and striking out again.

I asked to be transferred to the city. With Shanta gone, I felt freed of a beautiful burden. For a while I let myself adrift, submitting to the city's distractions. Once settled in the city I found no compelling reason for being there: it was like changing from one foot to the other.

I met my brother Basu. He was resting under an ivi tree in the heart of the city, looking old and withered. He lifted himself from the bench and came toward me in a trance. I let him embrace me. Looking down on the ground and wiping his tears, he said:

—Anandi, my own brother, there's nothing in your life now.

According to Basu, he had made something of his life; I had nothing to look forward to. He started telling me about his ailments. Now he seemed like a man already dying. He wanted me to take him to a good doctor. Basu had become like Mother. I wanted to get away from him. I counted myself fortunate that I could still see and feel.

The boys wrote to me. They said they were saving to visit me. Already they knew what they wanted to be. Suneil was aiming for law, and Ved was going to be an accountant.

They came for Christmas a few years later. They had grown so quickly. They were tall and slick like a couple of tennis players. They horsed around the flat crying obscenities at each other in colorless accents. Their talk was all about communes. They told me about the radical activities of the Wellington youth. But what they described seemed like acts of vandalism to me.

I said farewell at the harbor. I watched them join the crew on the ship's deck. A band played on the wharf, and people bunched in knots around the red and white musicians who stood brightly against the drab corrugated iron of the warehouses. The ship edged past the islands of the harbor. The two figures in white shimmered on the deck. I felt an immense lightness in my body. My thoughts turned strangely to pilgrimages and wanderings in holy cities. The crowd began to disperse. I pulled a pair of sunglasses from my shirt pocket, and put them on, and walked along the waterfront.

Beginning of the End

—The boys have gone bush again? Lorna sent Grace a quick enquiring glance and filled her glass.

Grace sighed, holding the wine glass with both hands.

—Sidney saw it coming. Mo brooding in the corridor, hands deep inside his sulu pockets. When he changes to his sulu you know it's coming. This time he took Master Josefa with him.

—What did Sidney say?

—Wonder how they'll manage to climb down the valley with this cyclone hovering so close to the island. Sidney has two extra classes, of course. But he says we can't be the judges. He's right. Perhaps it's the call of tradition or something.

—Bushwhacking! How do they say it, *"Sa lesu i na butobuto,"* Lorna retorted with the expression of someone who has the right to say outrageous things.

A chosen group had been invited to Stephen's house in the Domain after his Institute lecture. The lounge was half-full: a row of closed doors on one side, the back arched to join the circular front with large glass windows. All the furniture was removed from the center and piled against the wall between the doors and at the back wall. Some brightly colored mats and pillows were thrown on the floor. The walls were decorated with flowers and Pacific artifacts. On the front wall, above the bookcase, was a large polished turtle shell.

—I must find David, Lorna excused herself and squeezed past a circle of guests.

I saw her gliding away in her dull pink shirt and flayed white pants, exchanging greetings with the newly arrived couples who were deciding which knot of people to join. Lorna made an observation, but she moved away laughing before she was challenged.

Grace turned to Mrs. Morgan, a stout part-European woman. A shiny handbag dangled from her plump arm.

—Friday morning I came out on the balcony to watch the sun on the roofs. I'd done that for three years. Just then a PWD truck arrived on the front street. Four workmen jumped out. They took off their shirts, tied them around their necks, picked up their shovels, and started digging the road. Slowly and deliberately, as if they were preparing the ground for a lovo. I couldn't see any potholes or bumps, or broken pipe, but still they were digging up the road. The shovels clanged against the solid asphalt. I said to myself, something isn't right, they're digging up a perfectly good road. I watched their sweating bodies, listened to their graceless laughter. Then I turned away. I asked Mrs. Ram next door. She giggled and said the road will have a new name.

At mid-day I looked in again. The men had camped. They were drinking tea under a tarpaulin. The slush from their boots was everywhere on the grass at the edge of the lawn, the mud seeping in like paint.

Sydney, red-faced, blushing quickly, clad in white shorts and a shirt with flaming hibiscus, appeared at the door. His eyes caught a strange figure sleeping under a red and blue blanket by a window. Sydney smiled to himself and stared across the hall.

One of the closed doors opened, and Stephen emerged in his bright batik. He had a bald, aggressive forehead, gaunt face, and a well-cropped graying beard. Sydney moved jauntily toward him, and shook his hand. Stephen greeted him briefly and turned away as if his attention had suddenly shifted. Sydney withdrew to a corner.

The same door opened again and Salome came out wearing a shimmering cocktail dress which seemed at odds with her Afro and her rimless glasses.

—We must talk later, Lorna returned, and touched my elbow. I was inquisitive.

—But right now you'd want to meet the others. You must remember you are Stephen Riddle's chosen. I mean Stephen Bush's, she smiled enigmatically.

—Chosen like him? I pointed to the prostrate figure under the blanket.

—That's Dog. Dogett. I prefer to call him Dag. He's a volunteer.

Dog snorted and threw off his blanket. He tried numerous postures: he reclined like a mogul, squatted like a yogi, and finally coiled under the blanket like a fakir, his red paws sticking out.

—He looks awful, I said.

—Thank goodness he isn't wearing his battered khaki jacket. He's just overworked. Used to be attached to Health, and now they've put him in Forestry, and he has turned himself into a bush ranger. Dag's into Earth Life and that sort of thing. He has a great passion for preserving the rainforests. You might say Dag is an advocate of the tree, the same way Stephen is an exponent of the indigene.

An over-dressed couple waited at the entrance to be introduced.

—Oh, the Hortenses. Did you see them at the lecture? They've arrived this afternoon and were driven straight out to the Institute, and now here. I must say it's the quickest way to be initiated.

Shortly, Mrs. Hortense, who recognized Lorna, clamored to our side after stumbling over Dog's outstretched feet.

—Can you tell me who is Mr. John Thomas Self-Lalibangbang, and why I ought to know him? God, is he real? Is he? She gesticulated wildly.

Stephen, forlorn in the half-light, broke off from a group, loped to the center toward Mr. Hortense, and took him forward, waving his arm to attract Mrs. Hortense's attention in order to introduce them together. In this process various knots were broken. We switched groups. I found myself in the company of Tevita Kamu and a couple of university men. Kamu was holding court.

—I bought this house in the Domain, still heavily mortgaged, of course, Kamu emitted a short chuckle.

—I invited my M.P. friend for dinner and took him to the porch to admire the sea-view. He lit a cigar, and blowing the smoke in my face, said, now you have seen the sea-view, you can write poetry. Can you believe that?

—I sent him my first play which was inspired by my work with the Native Land Development Corporation. I know he didn't read it, otherwise he ought to have known I'm a playwright, not a poet. He told me once he never had to read a book after college. He was boasting of course.

Edward Nolte, a sociologist, who had the dishevelled appearance of a campus radical, received Kamu's comments with apparent enthusiasm, and ventured that writing was like dance and music, antidotes to corruption.

David drifted toward us with Mr. Malgehra. David's clothes suggested he had gone to bed in them.

—I've written reports for the government, among other things. But playwriting is what I want to do. It's like that in our country, your blood has something else and you end up doing what you can only do second-best. My friend, Anandi, will tell you.

Kamu threw his head back and laughed loudly, looking at the two academics, and pressing my hand warmly in both of his.

Ernest Small, the older academic, coughed politely to attract my attention.

—I suppose you are a local writer too? he asked in a controlled academic voice.

—No, I smiled. The only writing I have to show are some half-complete sentences in a notebook.

—I am told the half-complete lines are the beginnings of narratives. A book of half-lines! Seems an exciting proposition.

I wasn't sure how to regard his comments, but replied a little nervously:

—I'm for a diminutive form that should occupy one for a short time, without a beginning, and just the essential in between.

I felt foolish after saying that, and added quickly:

—I'll be content to be an M.P.

I saw Dog springing to his feet. After a few minutes he returned to his place with a mug of coffee, wearing a shirt and sulu. Kamu was speaking again.

—Some of us have to find time to sing to the drowsy rulers of the islands. But they hardly listen. My plays say things about the spoken tradition, the collective spirit of our people. . . . I know what they're saying about Mo and Master Josefa. They haven't gone into the bush to practice sorcery! How can we expect foreigners to understand? Some of our own people don't either. We have to express these things in writing. We have to flood our schools with our books. The average school teacher still has no faith in books by the local people.

Small's expression was disgruntled. He frowned at this unprincipled idea of literary pursuit.

Meanwhile, Mr. Malgehra, who had been trying to attract my attention, clutched my sleeve and drew me aside.

—I've always the greatest respect for the writing man. Background intellectuals. The government has a plan for a think tank. The Honorable Minister himself will tell you when he comes tonight. We can easily be the cultural marketplace of the world.

He offered me his tiny hand, soft like a child's.

—I don't believe we have been properly introduced before, he stared shrewdly at me.

Mr. Malgehra was a small, fair man with white hair. His rounded belly protruded through his silk Indian shirt. It was obvious he was one of those who provided the Party's victuals and fodder, which gave him his special kind of power.

I didn't like Mr. Malgehra. He had an aggrieved expression when he wasn't smiling, and he spoke in a whisper that made me uneasy.

I was rescued from him by a group of musicians who crossed the lounge, bowing and bowing. They filled the air with the sweet smell of frangipani that they wore in their hair. They started to strum their ukuleles.

Suddenly I found myself alone, caught out in the game of musical chairs. I heard Grace's voice. She was talking to Mrs. Hortense. Grace's quiet melancholic voice floated above the music.

—I stopped at the butcher's on my way to the school to pick up Sydney. I am half-time again at school, you see. The two Chinese butchers, smooth as ivory in that frosted shop, slid toward me. Their twinkling clear eyes always make me smile. They once showed me a photograph of themselves in silk Chinese costumes and pigtails. I thought how they seemed to have fallen from a pagoda into a cold chamber.

Grace's voice droned on, encouraged by Mrs. Hortense's silence.

—I found Sidney brushing white chalk on a parched playing field. The boy Luke was trying out the red flags in the corners. The principal had dozed off in his office. I don't know why I felt I'd break down and cry.

Brushing her tears and smiling, she continued:

—Sidney played the organ at the church when we first came here. Everyone said how well Mr. Hart played. Later when he started spending more time in the annex, I had the organ moved there so that he could practice. But he was always making things for the school with Luke.

I wanted to get away as far as possible from this lonely voice. My eyes searched for Lorna. She was perched on the arm of a sofa, holding a glass on her knee, listening the Mrs. Morgan. Lorna saw me and beckoned. I crossed the lounge to her. She smiled and continued to listen to Mrs. Morgan's palaver.

—The kitchen sink is full of dirty dishes and greasy pans, the children's bedroom is a mess. And there's June, curlers in her hair and a cigarette in her mouth, down on her hands and knees wiping up the floor, chattering all the time. She gets up only to pour herself a drop of gin. But if you met her at M.H.'s, she's a proper lady, precise in her speech and ways. Anyway, Lorna, I wanted to ask what's happening with your work permit?

—I've another project with the Arts Council. I'm more worried about David. Not about his work, you know. He has another year with the museum.

That's Stephen, now, said Mrs. Morgan. I guess he's off to the airport to fetch the Minister. Salome said he's returning from Papua New Guinea and straight here. I suppose that's all right, now that he's all by himself. That reminds me. I must have a word with Salome. Excuse me, dears.

She waddled away in search of Salome.

There was a mild altercation between David and Dog. I was glad Lorna didn't notice. Dog returned to his place again, and dropped on all fours on the mat.

—I was meaning to talk to you all evening. Let's go out on the porch.

Lorna finished the remaining wine in her glass. She picked up another glass as she went out.

The sky was gray and hot. It was like that before a cyclone. Lorna dropped into a reclining chair. We sat opposite each other without speaking. After a moment, staring into the night, she said,

—It'll be Diwali soon. And all those lights . . .

The shrubs behind her looked delicate and feathery in the dark.

—What did you think of Stephen's lecture? I asked.

Lorna raised her feet onto a small white table. The smell of perfume emanated from her body.

—What do you want? My comment on the scintillating phrase or the elements of surprise? I was asked before and I tried a summing-up line: the Galapagos of Stephen's mind transferred from Otago's fiordland to the barren plateaus of northern Viti Levu. Does that make sense?

—That's Salome's country.

—It's all tribal. Like Scots keeping the Sassenachs out. . . .

She took a large gulp from her glass.

—Don't knock Stephen's speech though. It's bound to be a blueprint of some sort. Did anyone tell you the story? I'm in the mood anyway. And so an unusually inward-looking chieftain springs up about a low hilly country in the north, growing maize and watermelons. A rich orchard appears in the dried-up river bed, and suddenly the ruins of the old village are filled with green. Everyone in the government is impressed. No one worried too much about the xenophobic attitudes. Everything was going so well. But Stephen wasn't satisfied with that, and he did the stupid thing—he found pieces of pottery, and claimed he had found a buried world. They turned out to be fragments from an Indian burial site. . . .

Lorna drew her breath.

—Now the other side of the story. Salome was earmarked for something big. The women's organizations here predicted they had a leader at last after she returned from Washington. But she gave up sociology and started searching for medicinal plants. That took her to the northern country, where she met Stephen, and was greatly inspired by his work and ideas. It wasn't really their marriage that scandalized government people, rather his meteoric rise. It was bound to be seen as a svengali thing.

Lorna inhaled deeply again looking into my face.

—I don't know why I'm telling you all this. I'm a little drunk, so you have to forgive me.

—What do you think Stephen expects from me, Lorna?

—You ought to know. You're a free agent, marginal, from the other side and not quite of it. Frankly, I think you'll make a good organizing secretary. And you need a strategy for surfacing. Work is a good anodyne for loneliness, as they say. Surely there's something you want to set right. Here's your great opportunity.

—I feel like I'm in a blind corner. I suppose when a man's copulative relation ends, he becomes a missionary or a politician. I guess I'll be an M.P. I need to meet a missionary. Shall I talk to Syndey?

—Did you see the toothbrush in his back pocket? His ears look so old!

After a pause, she said wistfully:

—You didn't ask what I'd like to do. I'd like to teach art and music to small children in a village. Does that sound romantic? But I think I'll end up owning a fashion shop, selling expensive dresses to the wives of government ministers at exorbitant prices, she laughed brightly.

A car stopped in the driveway. Stephen opened the door for the Minister. After him a tall Indian in a gray suit also stepped out. The Minister wore a blue suit and dark glasses. He broke into a laugh as he entered the lounge. The musicians stopped playing and started clapping. Others started clapping also. Stephen guided the Minister into a room for a short rest.

—Did you say hello to John Thomas? Lorna asked.

—I tried to talk to him. He says so little.

—Then you have to keep your eyes open. Didn't Stephen tell you? My goodness, how I have gone on without telling you what I really wanted to say.

I almost dreaded what she might say. I looked out into the night.

—I care a little, Anandi. Not much, mind, she smiled. There was something in Shanta's last letter that made me want to speak to you like this.

My eyes returned to her face. She rose abruptly.

—There wasn't much to say, was there? Let's get inside.

I decided to assess her words later. I followed her into the hall. The tall Indian, a United Nations expert, was still shaking hands all around and describing his journey to Funafuti.

—... alone in the whole jet with four air hostesses. Most frightful experience. Then I discovered I wasn't altogether alone. There was a fly dancing about my face. I yelled at the air hostesses. All four came running up the aisle. I showed them the fly. They giggled and said there was a buffalo on the plane.

The Indian guffawed raucously.

—And so I traveled to Funafuti with four air hostesses and one buffalo in a jet. I looked for the buffalo at the Customs but couldn't find him, he burst out again.

The Minister came out of the room looking rested. There was activity in the kitchen. For the first time Jemaima, the house girl, made her appearance with two helpers. The aroma of boiled food and spiced curries filled the lounge. The circles opened, and we drifted toward the table.

Mr. Malgehra strutted to my side.

—It was so interesting listening to Mr. Bhandari. Good sense of humor.

He filled my plate and helped himself to some salad. He steered me to a corner to discuss the Party's chances in the election. He nudged me on the side, and winked at me.

—It's good to see Dr. Stephen has a place for Indian food.

Stephen was seated with the Minister. The Minister ate with his fingers, making all the eating noises, chomping and inhaling. His mouth gleamed with perspiration and fat as the gastric juices hissed over balls of spiced food in his stomach.

A ripple of laughter from the musicians attracted our attention. They were playing more keenly now, and urging a young man to the center. The youth, a Samoan, was pushed forward. He started reluctantly, looking back at the musicians with a threatening expression, and soon amid encouraging cheers and clapping, he began a vigorous siva. We converged to the middle with our plates. Another youth joined him, twitching and jiving. Almost spontaneously Salome swayed to the middle, her hands stretched out, a plate in one hand. Her body rocked gently around the first youth. There was more shouting. She made her way to Stephen, trying to drag him in. Stephen, who was smoking nervously, frowned. She placed the plate with the remains of a fish head in his hand, smiled, and glided dreamily to the center. The dancers responded to the accelerated twanging and clapping. Salome threw her head back. Her body quavered with hidden energy. The Minister broke away from Stephen and wagged toward the dancers. The audience applauded. But he lost his balance quickly, and limped away merrily, wiping the sweat off his face with a handkerchief. Salome wriggled her way to Stephen again. She hugged him firmly, and cried:

—Happy birthday, Stephen!

The bubble of voices, which had started to die down, raised a fresh burst of cheers. Glasses were filled again. One of the musicians wheeled a large cake, already lit, toward Stephen.

July 10: Here I am then, garlanded, tilaked, poised like a deity. I'm in my own constituency where victory is assured. There are no issues. I'm describing minareted cities, sacred forests, deep-chested rivers fed from snowy mountains. My audience is a mangled reminder of another time. The headman, my right hand man, is lost in the nostalgic pleasure of the words. Some of the men are gazing at me like timid animals. They are seated on makeshift benches in the open shed erected for the previous weekend's wedding: remains of crepe paper decorations and twisted coconut fronds are still visible. The ground is strewn with sawdust. A pressure lamp hisses pleasantly. The women, silhouetted like ghosts, are on the shadowy veranda of the headman's wooden house. Behind the house, under the big mango tree, flocks of fowl are asleep in cages.

A lorry thumps on the uneven soapstone road, flashing its lights on the mottled hibiscus hedge.

I shift from one foot to the other, and begin on fables of hardship in the islands. Against these I posit the legends of horses of Turkoman, bred only in Merv and Khorassam. All this to prick the bubble with the matter of the war, and our shameful silence.

There's a ripple of protest, of course, but it's quickly subdued.

It's strange being called "the enemy of the people." There is no terror in it for me, though I know I will not be forgiven always. I'm sowing seeds of discord, it's said, but I say what I have to. There are allies like me in the Party who are chosen to be eliminated.

Now I see the need to have real enemies. Enemies keep you alive and on the look-out. My colleague Anthony Mahabutt, who was taken into the Party with me, said he had the same reason as I had for joining: to serve the people. But Mahabutt had the advantage of having enemies and scores to settle. How lonely it is to be without a sense of brotherhood, and how terrible to be without enemies.

There's a great hubbub after my speech. I am happy the Party stalwarts show satisfied expressions. Certainly they seem more enthusiastic than they were at the previous week's "Constitutional Guarantees," which caused one newspaper to predict that I was abandoning ship and turning Independent.

It's past midnight. My close supporters have arranged a celebration. We are slumped around a wooden table. There are scatterings of hangers-on about the shed. The headman roars orders to the women. I notice that his voice has a raucous edge. He is large and boorish, and has the blustering manner of a self-made man. When everything is in its proper place, he settles down opposite me.

Suddenly he becomes effusive, pours a couple of quick glasses of rum, and pauses to watch me gulp the hellish stuff down. My throat burns. I blink. The headman brays.

The confused babble of political chatter around me becomes uncontrolled, one voice on top of another. The headman's eyes turn bleary. He sticks to me like a leech, causing others to withdraw. But I feel kindly toward him. He has a hospitable voice. He prattles on about the wedding. About the food offering to his mother—he delivers a discourse on the sacredness of the Mother Principle.

And suddenly he has a question for me:
—Will our end be in a sinking ship?

It is a political question. He has heard rumors, bad rumors, about the fate of our community.

—Everything came of the ocean, all things will end there, I replied.

He seems greatly impressed with my reply. My eyes are drooping with exhaustion and drink.

A boy tip-toes behind the headman. At the same time his wife appears at the lean-to kitchen, straightening her sari. He staggers groggily toward her.

I can hear jangled music in the distance, and the nocturnal pounding of kava for a solitary drinker. From one of the huts, a hurricane lamp appears. Holding it is an old man. A dog whimpers. The old man brings the lamp close to his eyes to scrutinize the darkness. The light flickers. After a while he hobbles inside.

There is clucking and squawking behind the headman's house. The mango tree is strangely agitated.

The headman returns rather shamefacedly. Another bottle of rum materializes, heaven knows from where. My eyes turn toward a figure who has been in the half-light for some time. I recognize him immediately. I had seen him wandering in ill-fitting clothes, eyes perpetually downcast. Suddenly, he comes out of the shadow and stands at the table, grinning like a half-wit. It is his rum on the table.

I'm overcome by an overwhelming desire to escape. I cannot move: the headman is holding my hand in a vice-like grip.

Finally, avoiding the headman's farewell hug, I hurry into my car and drive away. A gentle haze is spreading over the skyline. The car moves pleasantly on the damp gravel. The air feels crisp, and there's fresh dew on the foliage. I can hear the soft breathing in the shrubs.

I'm relieved the lounge is just as I left it. The house has already been burgled twice. First everything was taken except the food. Next time they ate the food and defecated on the carpet, and wrote "Dog" on the mirror.

I sit in the toilet for a long time feeling a streak of vomit in my throat. I wash my arms and trunk in cold water, and curl up in a fetal position in the bed, pulling the bed cover over me to close out the morning light.

A drunken murmur fills my head. It's difficult to stop thinking when I'm in this condition. I try to re-order the half-complete thoughts and begin from the beginning. But always I find myself in the middle of something. I'm summoned to the Patriarch's office. To be sized-up, turned upside-down. Instead he receives me like someone who has already been chosen for an important role. His bearing has a hypnotic effect. Within seconds he raises my self-esteem. He seems to know everything about me: my frenzied anti-colonial speeches at the Indian University, my debating shield, my prize-winning essay on Nehru, and much more. Then he describes his own dilemmas, the sychophants who surround, the groveling sort, men without vision, who have nothing to offer except their servitude. Times have changed, he tells me. There are some problems which tradition can solve. Others require a modern approach.

He takes me in his limousine to a barrack-like hall. This is the haunt of a dissentient group. They're the newly educated, worried about their identity and place. They're drinking at a small bar in front of the dimly lit hall. The rest of the hall is empty. The Patriarch addresses them in their own language in a soft mystical voice. There are one or two cynical smiles. They aren't impressed with the notion of the ship of state requiring loyalty and devout leadership. But through simple incantation—I shudder at the power in his voice for mass hallucination—he seduces us into age-long dreaming. He describes with great certainty, in flashes of poetry, our reality in this universe and the realities of other people. He's shrewd. He knows that the habit of daily life is on his side, and that, for the moment at least, blood is thicker than politics.

The limousine glides swiftly through the dark street. The Patriarch smiles indulgently. Such an astute reconciler! I realize that, in our own disordered way, we've stumbled upon the fact that words are the great shapers of reality, and it's our destiny, of the privileged few, to shape the consciousness of our people. When the car stops he extends his hand toward me. I hold his long brown fingers eagerly. He smiles without speaking, and withdraws his hand.

In the months that follow, we make many journeys together, a couple of times deep into the bush. The land rover rumbles over the bad road. The Patriarch, so noble, stares out the window at the dull bush with the owner's eyes. We approach a village. First the smell of burned coconut fronds, then the pleasing lemon grass. It's a special kind of encounter. We're welcomed at the hidden village with ceremonial speeches and feast. But nothing is said about the purpose of our visit. There's an understanding that surpasses anything commonplace. We're genuinely saddened, my sadness heightened by the deep hospitality, when we say farewell.

Too many things happen together: people, speeches, trips to the far corners of the islands, all crammed into a single moment in time. At headquarters there's too much excitement. We're all entangled in the passions of the moment. Bits and pieces of news trickle in all day. Every bit from Mahabutt's mouth becomes important: numbers at meetings, factional troubles on the other side. I hold the notes in my hand and gaze at Mahabutt's angry eyes, the taut veins on his clear forehead. Ata comes to our side from the dissentient group. There are photographs in the newspapers—our photographs, selected to project our youth and aggressive intelligence. We take time off to admire them. We celebrate at headquarters, shouting: "Politics is a seductress, a repulsive bitch, and it's in our blood."

And alone in my apartment, like an exhausted actor who has played against his nature and interest, I ask: Have I been wrong again? The fear creeps in, What if the words we have uttered should create something dangerous and release it amid our people? We aren't mimics, I tell myself—we've hacked our way out of the bush, all of us—Ata, Mahabutt, and myself—and we are where we are in our understanding and control of reality. We cannot do anything else.

Sometimes I feel like the god Shiva who, after a thousand years under the sea, comes up to find the world has already been made: there's nothing more for him to do. So he tears off his genitals and heads toward the mountains.

August 15: Periodically, Stephen comes to us, like an unfortunate bearer of ill tidings, with bad news. He traces the disaster spots like an amateur sleuth. This time he has a vision of holocaust for me, masked in an apocalyptic language: strangely painted bird-like machines whirring over the islands, finding their targets, and swooping down on the sinking survivors like avenging birds, leaving behind charred stone and concrete and smoking trees. There are soldiers amok in the market place. The pigeons stalking the asphalted car parks clap their wings and take flight. There's blood on the footpaths.

It's not my vision of terror. I'm unsettled by other aberrations. My sleep is troubled by the bent old man scrutinizing the night mist: what fear or strife did he find lurking in the ragged night?

December 3: A burst of December rain leaves the streets wet and gleaming. The city is deserted. Everyone has driven off to the park for a football match. From the window of a restaurant I see a man closing the door of a photographic shop. He has difficulty locking the door. He looks over his shoulder at a passing taxi. His face seems familiar. I stroll toward my car, still gazing at the man. He sees me and turns abruptly. I find myself running across the street toward him. He cries out my name and literally lifts me off the street onto the pavement. He locks me in his arms, gazes at me from arms' length.

He opens the door of the photographic shop and invites me inside. The studio is shaped like a camera obscura. A circular hole cut in the wall serves as an entrance to a cubby hole from which glows a faint red hue. We sit opposite each other at a white table and talk for a long time. He has so much to tell me. Within a few minutes I learn all about his adventures since leaving the village, his life as a police photographer, and now the owner of this photographic shop. I continue staring at his face. There aren't any scars. He's almost handsome.

Abruptly he gets off his chair and takes me through the rounded entrance into the cubby hole. He finds me a stool, and from a shelf he draws out two photographic albums. Without saying a word he puts them on my lap and withdraws into the studio. I hear him making a phone call.

I recognize the first album immediately: photographs mounted on thick black paper between cheap boards. I turn the leaves quickly and pause at the photograph of the girl with the radiant laughter. The second album is leather-bound. It's full of old ghosts too. I'm filled with the pleasure of memory. The old photographs bear the imprint of the original owners. Some are inert and banal, some whimsical—the village caught in its rustic embarrassment. There's an especially poignant one of Mr. Nambiar's funeral. Following these are images, in color, of a new village: wooden and concrete houses on a freshly-leveled hillside, a small garage and taxi stand by the creek. In some photographs Mansa Ram appears in various parts of the village with a young woman, and with Emmanuel, his assistant.

The old and the new photographs are sublty contrasted and sequenced to express a life. I lean back and close my eyes, and return to the first album, to the photograph of the girl at the water's edge.

Mansa Ram returns after a while. He's grinning. In his hand he's holding a framed photograph. He places it in front of me. It's Mansa Ram and the young woman of the previous photographs. Her face is clearer, and at once the laughter of the girl's face and a fragment of it on the young woman's cheeks come together. I look up at Mansa Ram. He's sitting on the edge of the desk, smiling.

The sun comes out again as we set off together to meet Maya.

Glossary

apna-praya: "us and them."
arkathi: a recruiter of plantation workers.
badmash: wicked; disobedient.
barsati: a raincoat or slicker.
basti: a dwelling; village.
batik: a cloth print.
bhajan: a devotional song; hymn.
bhang: an intoxicating drug made from cannabis sativa.
bidi: a home-made cigarette.
bo ni bogi: a night flower.
bula: a Fijian greeting.
bure: a Fijian house.
casuarina: a tree or shrub with cone-bearing branchlets and needle-shaped leaves.
chamarin: a leather-worker's wife; a low-caste person.
cheelum: a pipe for smoking.
dalo: a tropical crop with a bulb-like root which is cooked and eaten.
dholak: a drum.
dhoti: a loin-cloth.
dilo: a nut with a smooth marble-like shell.
evuevu: a flowering coastal plant.

fakir: a mendicant or hermit.
fale: a Samoan house.
frangipani: a tropical plant bearing sweet-scented, star-shaped flowers.
ganja: Indian hemp, smoked for intoxication.
garandilla: passion fruit with a hard shell.
gasau: a wild reed used in building homes and fish fences.
gharry: a carriage or cart.
Gita: Bhagwadgita, the theological episode from the Mahabharta.
guava: a sweet tropical fruit.
hizra: a eunuch.
ivi: a Tahitian chestnut tree, with a heavy trunk and thick crown-bearing edible kidney-shaped fruits.
jahaji: a ship-mate.
Kali Puja: the worship of the goddess Kali.
kassava: a tropical plant with slender roots, cooked and eaten like dalo.
kava: a mildly intoxicating drink made from the root of the kava plant.
lali: a wooden gong beaten with two sticks.
lathi: a stick or club.
lavalava: a wrap-around garment worn like a skirt.
leka: little people.
liana: a climbing, twining tropical plant.
lota: a brass mug.
lovo: an earth oven.
machaan: a raised platform or scaffold.
mandali: a gathering for prayer or recital; an assembly.
mandup: a pavilion or shelter.
mekes: a Fijian ceremonial dance.
mela: a fair.
memsahib: a European lady.
minah: a dark, noisy tropical bird.
misnari: a missionary.
muraina: a weed found in rice paddies.
nati: a grandchild.
orhini: a headcloth, also used as a veil.
Panchayat: a meeting held for the purpose of arbitration.
pandanus: a palm-like tropical plant with sword-shaped leaves.
paragrass: a long, stringy grass.
puri: unleavened cake, fried in oil or butter.
roti: leavened or unleavened bread.

sadhu: a holy man or mendicant.
Sahib: a European man.
saijan: a fine-leaved vegetable.
salusalu: a garland.
sanyasi: a recluse; a hermit.
sari: an outer garment worn by Indian women; young, unmarried women wear saris only on special occasions such as weddings.
sarodh: a musical instrument similar to a violin.
sirdar: the headman or leader of a group of cane cutters.
siva: a Samoan dance.
sulu: a wrap-around garment worn by Fijian men; the same as a lava-lava.
talasiga: a dry region.
tamarind: a cultivated tropical tree with sour-tasting fruits; the juice is used as preserves.
tilak: a mark made on the forehead for ornament, or to indicate sect.
topee: a tropical hat.
tulsi: a basil plant.
virahdukha: the pain of separation or parting.
voivoi: a cultivated pandanus-like plant with serrated leaves used for making mats and baskets.
Yamduta: the messenger of death.
yaqona: a drink from the kava root.

About the Author

Subramani was born in Labasa, Fiji. His father had come to Fiji as an indentured worker. "Like many of my generation," says the author, "I grew up in a society in which people did not read books for pleasure. My interest in writing came from fortunate early encounters with books. We read some religious texts in Hindi, mainly Indian epics, and I tried some books in English through my father's encouragement, though he himself couldn't read English. The books we read had been thrown away at the European bungalows where my father worked."

Subramani was educated in Fiji and at the University of Canterbury in New Zealand, graduating with a B.A. in English. He taught high school for two years and then studied for an M.A. at the University of New Brunswick in Canada. He took his Ph.D. from the University of the South Pacific, where he has been a lecturer since 1974. There he became actively involved with a group of Pacific writers in encouraging creative literature from that region. He edited their journal *Mana* from 1976-1978. In 1979 he edited a centennial volume entitled *The Indo-Fijian Experience.*

Subramani's short stories have been published in a number of journals and anthologies. In 1978 his short story "Marigolds" won the South Pacific Association of Commonwealth Literature and Language Studies' short fiction competition. In the following year, "Gamalian's Woman" was a highly commended short story, as was "Dear Primitive," in a European short story competition. Apart from short fiction,

Subramani has written many critical essays, and is the author of *South Pacific Literature: From Myth to Fabulation* (1985), a study of Oceanic literature in English.

Subramani has been asked at various times to serve in the University of the South Pacific administration. From 1980-1983 he was Dean of Academic Affairs and more recently a Pro Vice-Chancellor. He teaches in the Department of Language and Literature and holds the position of Reader in English. Currently he is editing a book on narrative processes and is working on a novel about Fiji.

Set in the Asian Indian community of Fiji, the stories of *The Fantasy Eaters* deal with the ways in which transplanted Indian traditions alternately nurture and suffocate. The protagonist in "Marigolds," growing old in a state of alienation and anomie, laments the failure of his cultural compass: "A hundred years of history on these islands has resulted in wilderness and distress."

Stylistically, the cultural dislocation is rendered through the limited perception of the narrator. Thus, the reader is alerted to the fact that he is seeing only a partial reality. In the novella "Gone Bush," for example, the narrator's companion slips out of the story without explanation. This quality of people slipping in and out of view is very troubling—and very life-like.

Or consider "Tell Me Where the Train Goes" and "Tropical Traumas," two stories about cross-cultural sexual involvement with violent consequences. Each story is told from the point of view of an outsider whose own cultural limitations at once allow him a fresh perspective on the situation and blind him to the internal complexities.

Sober, formal, even pessimistic, the prevailing tone might sound foreign to American ears as much for its mature sensuality as for its unerring instinct that the most important things in life are sacred and fiercely resistant to scrutiny. Yet, first simply in the stories, then with rising tide in the novella, Subramani's vision of sickness in paradise—in body and body politic—is strangely more reassuring than naive optimism.